The Indigenous Species

John Gulbinas

Table of Contents

Dedication

I dedicate this book to all those who stand up for the advancement of humanity, cast away our old ways of conflict, war, and promote negotiations towards peace and preservation of earth.

Acknowledgement

I would like to thank Nancy McDougall for proof reading my story and giving me positive feedback.

I would also like to thank my son James who also read the story and suggested that I was light on descriptions.

My step daughter Wendy also proof read my early editions and gave me valuable inputs.

About The Author

The author wrote a short story and his English teacher told him he should write a book.

This concept followed him throughout his life and in the back of his mind, added to it.

Over many years in became this story. After working as an aerospace engineer, business developer, finance director, along with extensive travel, he searched for a view of the really big picture and where we are all heading.

Goal of This Story:

To provide a new perspective of our planet and human development from an alien viewpoint. A morally and intellectually advanced species arrives, preventing hostile takeovers from other aliens, and reviews human development to decide which species can best preserve and enhance the planet. The supreme species of the universe developed over millions of years in a challenging multidimensions environment.

Humans have become detached from the Earth. Business, finance, and economics are concepts that have made Humans disconnected from Earth's land, sea, atmosphere, and life forms. Humans show a profit with no accounting for the destruction of resources. Why the lack of happiness and fulfillment? Why do children easily play with foreigners but grow up with prejudice even without ever meeting the other side?

Species 1000 gives humans an intellectual chance for redemption. Failing this is a fighting chance, with one-on-one combat against aliens in strange planetary settings.

Humans can use all the capabilities of Earth's creatures to enhance their combatants. These human fighters become extreme fighting machines after major surgery. Intelligence is key in analyzing the weakness of other life forms. Training in massive gyms takes place against rhinos, elephants, lions, giant crocodiles, and robots.

Earth loses its first several battles. Hawaii is taken over by aliens. Then Australia is lost. Humans watch as aliens enjoy and enhance our continents.

Drastic measures are taken on Earth – population control and severe environmental restrictions.

Battles occur on strange planets: some have rain falling like daggers and bricks, others on twin planets where the combatants can jump between the two small planets. Battles on gas planets. Battle under extreme gravity against pool like creatures. Strange off-planet settings show how fortunate we are on Earth.

Earth's combatants endure extreme surgery, including a third rear eye, taken from a young boy who willingly offers it but then becomes totally blind. Aliens step in to help the poor child.

Earth's H33 combatant begins to win. Earth's nations pull together, led by a young leader pushing for drastic change.

Elizabeth's PHD work on stress training is used on H33 to enhance his ability to deal with extreme mental challenges.

H33 has 4 wins, allowing Earth to occupy another planet. Planetary options are presented from a menu – choices are not appealing.

The Alien 1000 leader, Sam, gives us a perspective on their species' evolution and on an even more advanced species that gave up all to live on the edge of the growing universe.

The human race shows promise only when pushed to the brink, but will they be granted indigenous rights to continue? What steps will the Alien species 1000 take to preserve Earth?

Author's Notes:

This short story, written over my lifetime, came from a love of science fiction and the perceived need to impact how we view our planet and the human species. Environmental issues need a new perspective. We don't have a central body controlling the planet. We don't have a focus on advancing the human race. I try to bring these topics alive.

We are unlikely to defeat aliens capable of reaching our planet. Humans have overwhelmed less advanced indigenous species – is alien takeover inevitable?

What if a very advanced alien species gives us the chance to prove ourselves by preventing a hostile takeover? What questions would they ask? Do we need an outside competition to bring us together? What sacrifices would we be willing to make?

The Aliens in control push us to advance our species using resources from all Earth has to offer. The combatants undergo enhancement surgeries. Sons offer precious organs sacrificing sight. Psychological battles from within. Heroes step up. Humans try to change - not fast enough. The Aliens analyze our cancerous tendencies and path towards self-destruction. They learn to read our brain waves. Options for Earth are evaluated. What went wrong in Earth's development? Can a new brand of leaders work together and make the difficult choices?

Now the story begins . . .

Future Earth

Elizabeth's Big Day Interrupted

Elizabeth walks boldly on a stone path through the university campus with old Greek stone buildings contrasted with synthetic 3D printed buildings that look like architectural experiments. Elizabeth, now 27, sports a retro look uncommon in someone her age and gets noticed. She wears a graduation-inspired grey and white outfit she hopes will encourage the professor to grant her Ph.D. She is walking with a few antiquated books in her hands, cradled to her chest. An implant in her forehead displays a hologram of the professor she is about to meet. Softly she says, "Time," and the heads-up display shows it's 9:50 am June 2, year 3024. A notice flashes 10 minutes to her appointment.

Elizabeth thinks back to when she started this study of intense conflicts. Wondering why she ever became so interested in the subject. Fascinating to her, yet she can think of no source of inspiration from her past or from a disposition maybe because her mind is so even-keeled and continuously calm that she is intrigued by this unknown. Next to her is a computer-generated friend that appears very real. She speaks to it, "I really hope I am awarded a Ph.D. today and that Professor Flanagan does not think me strange.

He is a good man and honestly cares. That is why I have gone the extra kilometers on this thesis."

She continues walking across a grass-filled landscape with tall trees making her way to a now ancient university building. As she enters a majestic hallway with stained glass windows, she looks up towards the skylights, then down the long hall. At the end of the hall, she sees a large synthetic wood-like door with the holographic image, "Professor of Psychology and Human Endeavor."

Elizabeth knocks on the door at a distance without touching it and it automatically opens. She is scanned. "Interesting books you have there," says the professor. "Vintage editions with the added pleasure of turning real pages. But we are here for something far more important: your final dissertation. Come in and please take a seat."

Elizabeth comes in, shy but confident, puts down her documents and her implant connects to the holographic screen in front of them.

Elizabeth begins, "My Ph.D. application thesis is on the long-term psychological impact of conflict and the mental recovery process. Those sent into combat, or similarly high stressed environments, have post-traumatic symptoms that vary based on the intensity and duration of the conflict. The effects can be reduced by pre and post-conditioning. I have devised several means of conditioning prior to high stress conditions and have also devised post treatments. All conditioning methods have been tested and the results documented."

Professor Flanagan comments, "Conflicts of this magnitude rarely occur today. As a society, we are reducing the incident rate every year. However, I find this study of the extreme very useful in addressing common stress environments and the case studies provide perspective on social and occupational struggles." He starts to review the executive summary and case study results.

His eyes widen, and he sits back, startled by the studies. "Elizabeth, these case studies have a shocking level of stress factors. Where did you find such individuals in crisis?" Pictures appear on the screen with men, women, and teens in distress, each labeled with their issues.

Elizabeth, "Mostly in and around the campus. Exam time, first-year arrivals, and those departing early. Also, faculty support staff, and seven educators."

"Seven educators?" Professor almost shouted in disbelief. "I really need to get out more."

Elizabeth tilts her head in partial agreement.

The professor continues now with peaked interest and a growing concern. "I see here that you devised training programs and measured hormone levels, heart and breathing rates over weeks – their stress levels came down very nicely.

Excellent work! I would love to sit down with some of these individuals and have them recount their experiences. Then I would back up your publishing of this research. Can you convince some of them to meet with me?"

Elizabeth, "Yes, I believe many would like to meet you."

Then on a private screen in front of the professor, a news break suddenly appears. The professor's eyes widen intensely as he focuses on the interruption. "What on Earth is this?" shouts the professor.

The news anchor speaks in a state of shock, "This is a restricted news flash to select individuals. A truly monumental event has occurred. Please prepare yourselves for what you are about to see is real and has been verified by NASA, Russian, Chinese, and European intelligence. The information is being released slowly to those in leadership and selected academics to prevent panic."

The professor's mood suddenly shifts to a state of alarm, and his back straightens, "I am very sorry, Elizabeth, but I have to take this notice immediately and we will have to reschedule. You will understand why shortly. This is Earth-shattering." Elizabeth leaves with a look of confusion – "What is going on?" she asks softly to her computer-generated friend as she walks out.

On The Other Side of the Galaxy

On a liquid methane planet, deep below the surface, lies a coral-like building with a strange sign. It cannot be read by humans but means 'Galaxy Planet Mining Operations – looking for new habitats'. An octopus-like creature sits inside on a mound with eight keyboards facing its eight arms. A 360-degree screen fills the room, and his eight eyes focus all around him, or is it her? It scans the universe and has a full range of signals on all frequencies. Planets are found, scanned, found void of life and dismissed one after the other. Some are filed as potential mineral reserves. The file for liquid-based habitable planets contains only three findings.

Then the creature jumps up from its mound. He has found a probe. The probe's trajectory is traced. The material of the probe is analyzed and aged. The level of advancement of the probe is translated to the rating of the species that must have developed it. The path back to its source is shown on the screen as a cone ever increasing in size until it is blocked by a black hole.

"Aha!" says the creature. "We had missed this one due to the black hole." Spoken in a gurgling underwater tone with clear breaks between words.

The creature starts typing on its keyboards quickly and messages come spooling back. Signals are sent out to their spaceships closest to the discovered planet. The closest ship takes charge and heads towards the newly discovered planet.

Another spaceship gets the notice, but it is further away. On board is a traitor. Its lover is from another species. The traitor sends the location to its lover and the location is sold to another aggressive species.

This aggressive species locks on the first spaceship going to the discovered location. The chase is on towards Earth.

Back on Earth, the Aliens Arrive

A newscast continues after Professor Flanagan has joined his council. They all watch a restricted news flash showing the arrival of alien species in Earth's orbit.

The news reporter begins, "Here is the scene taken from Earth's satellites." One alien spaceship arrives and begins to scan and launch cyber-attacks on Earth's defenses. One hour later, another alien ship arrives, having followed the first. It fires some unknown weapon that only shows as a blur and deflects off the first ship, which fires back into its shield. Then, a third more advanced ship arrives, and the firing of the weapons by the first two ships is somehow reversed in time.

The reporter continues, "Our scientists cannot explain this and have verified it is not a recording error or a hallucination, but seemingly a real time reversal. Here is some more footage from our satellites." The first two ships have been placed into plasma bubbles and have become inert, rotating around each other. Then they are moved to the far side of the moon. "We have received no communications. Radar systems have picked up some foreign elements entering Earth's atmosphere." Pause, "I am just getting word from military sources that the aliens have now tapped into our internet and undersea fiber optic cables and are accessing all our data. They have real time access to all our communication networks, including our most secure military databases. We wait and prepare the best we can. Please try to maintain calm and show others that we have retained our composure. We will continue to assess and prepare. More info will be provided as events unfold. Please set the example of calm and control to prevent widespread panic."

Movie Theaters Tapped To Learn Our Language

In movie theaters around the world, miniature fly-like probes enter and land softly on people's heads, unnoticed. The probes pick up brain waves along with the sounds and images on the screens. Massive amounts of data are transferred back to the advanced alien ship's computers that calibrate brain waves versus language versus images. The undersea cables are tapped with underwater drones. All wireless transmissions are being collected and sent to the advanced alien ship.

Military leaders become anxious, thinking they must move now before the aliens understand all our capabilities. They decide to launch fighters to get a closer look at the alien ship.

Russian, Chinese, and USA fighter jets are launched. They try to communicate with the alien ship by sending this message: 'Earth's defense units have been launched to protect this planet. Retreat immediately!'

As the advanced fighter jets get into the upper atmosphere and approach the alien ship, the planes simply turn back. The USA flight control towers ask their pilots, "Why are you turning back?"

The USA lead pilot responds, "Control tower, this is the lead fighter, Gama delta five, I have lost all control, the stick has no input, displays are functional, full power and oxygen but the plane is flying itself. The flight is stable. Attempting to regain control... attempting again... all attempts fail."

Russian and Chinese fighters simultaneously lose control of their jets. All fighter jets return to their bases. They land on their original airfields precisely without incident. Pilots all state that they had suddenly lost all control and yet their planes landed flawlessly with precision. The planes self-return to their hangers in a new denser pattern, taking a fraction of the space previously required.

The Russian president is furious and launches a new high-technology hypervelocity missile from a hidden base on the moon. Other countries are shocked – they were unaware of this hidden weapon. The missile is on track to hit the alien spaceship, but then control is taken over. The missile turns and heads towards Russia. The Russian space agency tries desperately to regain control. They cannot, and then they try to detonate the missile, they cannot. The Russians fire their anti-missiles towards it, but they are redirected, collide with each other, and explode. The Russian leader who had commanded the attack runs to his underground safe room.

The missile penetrates Russian airspace and continues to accelerate, its course now fine-tuned to the leader's exact location. The impact is precise, killing just him, and as the explosion expands, it reverses, imploding to limit the damage.

World News Broadcast

Rumors of spaceships in orbit come from those with high powered telescopes. This quickly becomes a reality on news broadcasts around the world. The world is buzzing with the news of alien ships. People react, asking for answers, not knowing what to do next.

The United Nations sends out a news report in harmony with every country. "We have an announcement that one of the alien ships in our orbit is now prepared to contact us in forty-four minutes. It appears that the 3rd alien ship that has arrived is in control and is completing an in-depth assessment of our internet database. Experts worldwide have stated that these spaceships are very advanced, and this third ship is by far the most advanced, having easily neutralized the other two ships. We have not seen any signs of aggression, but all military organizations are at the ready to defend our planet."

Nervous groups gather from around the world. Governments and military organizations communicate to gain some form of coordinated efforts, but all are ill-prepared. There has been no advanced agreement on how to proceed or who will take the lead. The method of attack and defense are disputed as they assess the level of technology displayed. The US military strategist and chief technology officer state, “We have seen just a brief glimpse of what they can do, and judging by the lack of any significant defense from the first two species, the third alien spacecraft is extremely advanced, and it is difficult to assess how we could have a military advantage. The way they neutralized our fighters was one thing. But to control the Russian missile back to the person who launched the order, then limit the damage to kill only him, is simply unbelievable. Obviously done to send a message that they will not be messed with.”

First Contact

The third alien ship sends out internet messages to all nations in text and voice, similar to their most renowned reporters.

“Hello, beings of Earth. I believe you call yourselves Humans. We represent the species 1000, which means we are the most advanced species in this section of the universe. Your internet and other databases have been very useful to our understanding of your history, culture and current events. We will prevent the immediate invasion and inhabitation of your planet by other species and thoroughly assess your situation. Military groups can relax as nothing they have can affect us. Your military technology rating is 40 versus our 1000. Consider the chance a cave period child would have against your military today, and you will begin to understand the implications. Your military arsenal is easily controlled by any visiting species and provides the resources they can use to eliminate you. You should review this situation. We will continue to assess and meet with your leaders to ask some important questions. Pick your representatives from each country wisely and prepare to meet us in forty-eight hours. We will provide the arrangements. Meanwhile, continue with your daily routines. The current situation is under control and will remain stable."

Leaders of each country are in shock. They call in their vice presidents, chief of staff, military leaders, and technology experts to discuss the situation. Who shall attend, how many should we bring? How do we secure the meeting? Each leader decides to bring in a technology adviser and a military leader.

The leaders become anxious. Now one hour to the meeting and no directions have been provided by the aliens. Comments come from their ready rooms, "How can we all meet within one hour?"

Forty-seven hours and fifty minutes. Still no answer. They become suspicious. One leader said, "Maybe they will attack us as we wait for a meeting."

At exactly forty-eight hours, the alien message appears, "Please depart and arrangements will be made on route." They go to their helicopters, limos, and planes, confused as they have no directions. As the leaders enter the door to their transport vehicles, they suddenly appear on a beach in a small island. Leaders from all countries appear one after the other. A warm, gentle breeze blows. Leaders are speechless as they look around at their surroundings and at each other.

Alien Negotiations

They wait anxiously for the arrival of the aliens. The leaders line up facing the ocean. Some nervous discussion occurs, “Is this real? Are we still on Earth?”

“Yes,” says the Prime Minister of Australia. “This is Earth and we are near the equator.”

They see something coming down from the sky. Very small, maybe it’s just a bird. It becomes larger and larger. It’s beautiful. Like a bird but human in shape, a beautiful pale blue. The shape of a beautiful girl but bird-like with fine wings that have many feather-like fingers. She flutters onto the beach, stumbling. Men jump to assist but stop, not knowing quite what to do. So, they back off. She smiles the most beautiful smile of peace and fragility. She struggles to stand, not accustomed to the gravity of Earth. Her breathing is rapid but enhanced by an apparatus strapped to her neck that quickly adjusts and she breathes a sigh of relief.

She speaks, “Can you understand me?” in a faint high-pitched voice that goes beyond their hearing range. “If so, raise your right arm.” They raise it slowly and only partially, as they have trouble hearing the faint speech. She repeats, “How about now? in a louder, clearer tone but with a bird-like texture, lower pitched than before but still feminine and soft. They raise their hand quickly and high. "Good," she responds.

The Earth's UN world leader speaks, "Welcome to the Earth! You are the first alien to arrive here. Are you comfortable here on our planet?"

The bird lady says, "Almost, but it will take some time to adjust to the light spectrum, atmosphere and weather. You have a glorious amount of water here," as she splashes her webbed feet along the beach. She sighs a beautiful note at the top of their hearing range and beyond.

Then she begins. "Two alien species have arrived to inhabit your planet, and many more will become interested. Your probes and signals were triangulated to your position and then sold. Your planet is one of the most, if not the most beautiful in the Galaxy. Mining for such pearls is a big intergalactic business. We are all here to ensure the planet will live a long and beautiful life. Our basic question is simple. Why do you believe that humans should manage the Earth? We have prevented a hostile takeover. These species will offer to return Earth to its jewel-like quality and enhance it beyond its original glory. We are overseeing the preservation of life, ensuring negotiations take a non-destructive path. Some species in your situation would decide to destroy their planets or poison them to prevent any new inhabitation. We prevent this and any other threats."

She stops and looks around at the plant life and notices a small crab running along the sand near the water. Then she looks up and continues, “Negotiations will take place with several alien species. We hope that you consider the different philosophies that you will face. The process will decide the outcome. In the event that our initial discussion does not lead to a solution, one on one combat will occur in a neutral planetary setting. This will demonstrate which species can best benefit from its planet’s gifts. Prepare yourself and your people. Your future is in your hands. Goodbye”.

Then she turns, flaps her wings quickly, runs along the beach, skims along the water, adjusts her wing angles to improve her flight, adjusts to the atmosphere and flies upward quickly into the sky.

The leaders turn to each other in shock. One leader speaks, “Not the battle we had expected.” Another says, “We should have had a contingency plan for this.” A third says, “And we all thought that our military might would save us against a species that can travel across the Galaxy. They can control our weapons better than we can. We even sent out invitations with our probes. Like ‘planets.universe@uz’. Come visit, stay if you like. It’s all free to the first aliens!” Some start to laugh. Then stop and say, “Wait, not funny.”

Leaders Return Post Initial Contact

The leaders arrive back home by stepping out of the vehicles they had just entered. Others around them ask, "Have you decided not to go?" The alien encounters have distorted their perception of time.

The leader says, "We have already met. I have returned."

Each leader informs their staff, "This will not be a military conflict. This species will evaluate us and give us a chance to maintain sole control of this planet. Any conflict will be one on one between competing species to prevent our planet's destruction."

Leaders from around the world have meetings with their top scientists, philosophers, environmentalists, and CEOs of the largest companies. Discussions are confused, as they don't know what to do or how to prepare. At the end of the discussions, the leaders of countries tell their extended staff to be ready to respond to anything the aliens may request.

Next Meeting: Let's Have Dinner

The leaders of the top nations and the UN are invited to a dinner. Microchip invitations land, delivered by various bird species (owls, eagles, doves, hawks, blue jays) indigenous to the leaders' countries. The species 1000 is attempting to avoid a strong military tone. Once played, the microchips state, "You are invited to dinner to discuss your achievements and future goals. Transportation will be provided. Be prepared within 48 hrs. You will not be harmed and will be returned after our 8-hour meeting."

All leaders are very nervous, wondering how to prepare and what security to bring, if any. A day passes. Nothing. They all go to work as usual, but when they open the door to their offices, they find they are all on the same island near the equator. They each have a place at a dining table made from local trees and vines, beautifully created with an alien attempt to replicate Earth like art. They wait, standing on the sand, looking at each other.

In the distance, they see something in the sky, as before. It is ice blue and diving towards them. Some move aside, thinking it is a missile or weapon as it is larger and coming in with greater speed. Then it opens up. It is a bird-like man – ice blue, feathers like fingers but very many. It is a male version of the lady bird-like creature. The alien lands on the sandy beach with ease, having adjusted to the atmosphere based on the previous encounter.

The male alien begins, “Welcome, leaders of Earth! Before we begin, I would like to ensure we have optimum communication in place. If you understand me clearly, raise your left hand. Okay, now lower it. Please take the beverage in front of you. It is a stabilizing agent to put all your body functions in their optimum range, so you will be able to understand and respond. You all show varying degrees of stress and this will remedy the problem. If we wanted to harm you, it would have been done. We could simply step aside and the first two species would destroy you.”

Reluctantly, they smell the beverage. It smells both amazing and natural. One takes it. He says it tastes like a smooth fruit punch. They all take the shot and look at each other. Facial tensions relax and they smile.

Alien says, “Excellent, now let’s begin. Your situation is this. The planet Earth was discovered by two species which arrived earlier. We represented the most advanced in this universe and arrived in time to prevent any hostilities.”

The creature stops to listen to a silent incoming message. Then continues, “My daughter just suggested that we introduce ourselves and provide you with names you can pronounce. You can refer to our species as 1000, which is the reference point for species’ developmental level in this sector of the universe. She has derived the following localized names, as you would not be able to pronounce or hear our own names correctly. She suggests Sam for me, Dawn for my wife, who you met first, Huston for my son, and JD for herself. I am sure that JD chose these names' local significance. Do you know what they would be?" No answer as they just look at each other.

Sam continues, "We have compiled all Earth's data on your history. Now we have many questions. We have also studied your brain waves and can communicate directly, but this may be difficult for you. The drink should help. No need to vocalize your response. Simply think clearly and we will understand you more effectively without the distortion caused by placing thought into language. Vocal and hearing distortions will be eliminated as well. As my wife Dawn mentioned, there are several alien species that would like to inhabit this pearl planet and they would promise to take excellent care of it. Human history shows that might is right and the superior species takes over to displace the indigenous species. People from Europe invaded North America and pushed aside all natives. This also occurred in Australia, Africa, and on many islands. Humans recontoured Earth's surface not unlike an alien species. You also wiped out many less advanced life forms. Human's right to control the Earth is not without question and invasion by a superior species has much precedence here."

"However, we would like to give you the chance to defend your position and maintain this planet via your indigenous rights, which our species aims to preserve in order to maintain diversity in the universe. Every avenue will be offered to you. We truly hope you can provide a sound argument and actions. All answers should consider the biggest picture and highest-level, long-term view."

"First question: What are the achievements of the human race? What type of organism are you? How do you compare to other species on your planet? What is your vision for the planet? Who rules the planet as a whole? How is the harmony created? What is the life expectancy of the human race? What is the intellectual, cultural and environmental development plan? Do you have an alien component? Given your history of wiping out native humans from many lands and using weaker races as slaves, would you see superior races from other planets doing the same?"

Sam stops and evaluates all their responses. Then continues, "Your responses are not in-depth or consistent among you. Perhaps you need time to digest the situation. Earth was developed with substantial harmony and self-preservation systems. The rain washes you and the planet naturally feeds you. Otherwise, you would die in your own waste. Your atmosphere protects you. The winds are calm, the rain is gentle. Earth is stable. None of this is a given on other inhabitable planets. Other species would pay a high price to inhabit this planet. Do you understand what a cancer organism is? That it consumes to excess with the destruction of its host and itself? All without purpose."

"Prior to our control, these alien species would have wiped out humans and taken better care of the Earth. (He pauses, then continues) We will return you now. Note, however that Human's right to control the Earth is not without question. You have already established the precedence for superior species to take control."

The leaders rematerialize in their offices at the end of the day. Others ask, "Where have you been?"

Reply, "To see the alien in charge of this sector of the universe, and... of our planet's future".

"How was it?"

"We are not in a strong position to answer their difficult questions."

Human's Common Dream

The next scene is at an outdoor café. One man is sitting, and his friend joins him. A pretty girl walks by. They both look at her like they know her.

One young man says, "That girl looks familiar. Wait, I had a dream last night and that girl was in it."

The other guy looks up, choking on his herbal drink and then looks more intently at the girl and then his friend.

The first man continues, "We were on a sailing ship being blown around the world. I grabbed a good spot on the deck. She was cold and alone, so I asked her to sit next to me. There was no one sailing the ship. People were fighting for the best spots on the boat while the ship narrowly missed rocks and icebergs. No one cared to steer the ship or ask where it was going. "

The other guy says, "Umm," and pauses. "I had the same dream."

His friend looks at him, "Stop messing with me… my mistake for talking about a dream."

The second man continues, "No, really, I had the same dream. This is freaky."

Then on the news later that evening, "Everyone is talking about a common dream across the nation. Psychologists are analyzing it to see if this is some form of joint hallucination or induced by the effects of an alien encounter or maybe even implanted by the aliens."

Over the next week, the dream is had by all over the age of 16.

Elizabeth also has the dream, but she is the girl, cold and alone on the ship. She is looking over the edge of the wooden ship and sees a dark sea looming. She feels death on the horizon, but she does not fear it. Instead, she studies it like part of her Ph.D. Scanning the horizon, she sees icebergs, whales, sharks, and storms in the distance. Objects that could destroy the ship and all on board. She goes back to the main deck and a man asks her to join him in a safe spot. She looks at him and hesitates. Then she awakes.

Human Leaders and the Best Intellects Gather To Answer the Alien Questions

After much discussion, one leader decides to create a chart on a holographic screen.

The structure of human endeavor is categorized and a chart is displayed:

Technology

- Arts
- Law and order
- Space and astronomy
- Physics
- Engineering
- Management
- Philosophy

As the leaders work this out and agree with experts in each field, the Alien Sam interjects.

"Your world is 66% ocean, 34% land. Over both, you have a layered atmosphere including ozone and magnetic poles for your protection. On land, you have mountains, rivers, forests, wildlife, etc. Why are so many of the items on this chart abstractions from the realities of your planet? These critical Earth elements are replaced by the struggle for economic power and wealth, leading to feudal infighting with the most aggressive taking leadership. Those in harmony are moved out, leaving a genetic pool with an increasingly warrior driven mentality without empathy for the Earth and its life forms, potentially dooming this planet."

Human Chart	Alien's Chart
Economy	Planetary impact and preservation
Business	Human advancement
Politics	Coordination of human efforts
Technology	Technology
Law and order	Ocean, plant and animal life
Engineering	Human resource development
Space and astronomy	Understanding the universe
Physics	Pollution abatement
Philosophy Arts	

Sam continues, "I agree with engineering, physics, space and your organizational activities, but technology should be tied to the elements of the Earth and your continued survival. Your whole notion of profit is puzzling. How can you have profit that causes the destruction of your planet? Any damage to the planet should be accounted for when it causes a permanent loss in resources. True profit would enhance the planet, life, harmony, and reduce pollution, improving your atmosphere. Healthy seas and rivers to swim in, with an abundance of fish. And most importantly, a sky filled with all species of bird (a bit of a joke there). Rain forests that grow would also be a nice touch. Your notion of development results in extinction, not preservation, and no creation of new species. It also reduces the overall quality of life by increasing stress and disease. I am asking for your views. Then, I will ask all humans and see if there are those who can comprehend this and sow the seeds to save this planet."

The leaders go back to the discussion and break off into smaller groups.

On Board the Alien Ship

Series 1000 aliens rest, hanging from their feet. They have two brains; one during the day takes care of all short-term activity and collects information. The night brain analyzes daily data and provides the day brain with its plan for the next day, looking after the long-term objectives and maintaining a clear path of action. These species do not know loneliness as they are always accompanied by their second brain. During the high demands of the day, the night brain can awake and provide extra capacity.

Family Time With the 1000's

Father Sam asks his daughter JD, "How did you arrive at our names?"

JD says, "Looking into Earth's history, I investigated their best leaders. I liked Abraham Lincoln. But you are not here to be their leader but to help create their leaders, so I picked his father's name, Samuel or Sam."

Sam replies, "Nice touch. I like it."

JD says, "Dawn for mother, was easy like the morning she is full of promise like the day ahead. Each morning reminds me of my mother." She pauses briefly, then goes on. "Huston is the location for the old USA control center for space activity and since my brother is the controls expert, the Earthlings would understand the name."

Sam, "Okay, but JD for your name is a puzzle."

JD says, "Well, dad, you know I am nature obsessed and I found someone, a spirit in history that wrote songs about nature on earth. These songs capture the beauty of Earth – here are some lines."

The music is played, "I have seen fire in the sky... take me home country roads... sunshine on my shoulders makes me happy." These are some of the best musical images of Earth and JD are the initials of the musician who wrote and sang them but eventually drove his plane into the sea.

Sam says, “Okay, but the humans I spoke to did not seem to get the significance.”

JD replies, “After some study, they will.”

The son Huston plays an old recording from NASA, “Huston we have lift off... Huston we have a problem.” Cool, I like my name now. Sounded weird at first, to pick a city name.”

Sam says, “Okay, let’s flock together and view the results.”

JD replies, “Flock. Really? We are not primitive birds of the Earth.”

Sam, “No harm in trying to fit in (with a bird smile).”

Son Huston's Evaluation Room

The bird son Huston maps the Earth's worldwide military in a 3D hologram model. As he scrolls his hands across the large transparent table, images appear of all Earth's weapons: jet fighters, missiles, nuclear subs, and troops. Playing with the model, he runs simulations of various war scenarios showing data on damage to the Earth, population loss, animal and plant life loss, and long-term impact on the planet. The results appear over Earth's image.

Looking into the future, Huston summarizes the probabilities of worldwide war and nuclear fallout. Then the key weapons to be neutralized.

Huston goes to see his father Sam with excitement about the cool scenarios for this planet. "Father, I have modeled this world's military and have run 1.3 million scenarios out to the local year 40600. Humans reach a maximum of 12% of our development before Earth becomes inhabitable. We have a very high-risk situation and the models tell me we should neutralize many military sectors and all nuclear weapons immediately to avoid an 80% loss in species."

Human development scenarios appear on the holograms and plots show the courses ending in the destruction or near destruction. Percentages of life forms remaining are shown by species type.

Huston says, "Human advancement is that of a 2-dimensional creature with a short lifespan. Future predictions show human activity is incoherent, uncoordinated and without a real long-term purpose."

Sam says, "Show me, son," and the summary is displayed. Dad makes some minor moves in the parameters and reviews the species and population loss. Dad's mind spins his second brain kicks in. His two brains communicate.

Huston says, "The results show that they indirectly accept that they are destroying their planet and, alongside, themselves, yet they continue the daily path that does not fulfill them. How can they feel fulfillment when they see no common vision driving them towards a better future on Earth or as a valuable part of the universe?"

Dad nods his wings to agree to nuclear neutralization. The son devises the nuclear neutralization equations and the father suggests catalysts to reduce the plutonium and uranium half-life.

Sam states, "Don't forget the tactical field devices". Son replies, "Yes, already done, Dad. Should I eliminate their refinement plants and neutralize their atomic mineral reserves?"

Dad replies, "Create a plan and let's review it together."

Daughter JD Meets Mother Dawn

JD asks, "Can I fly to their rainforest and take back samples to my lab?"

Dawn replies, "Okay, but bring a defense drone and level one protection."

JD says, "Really, I can take care of myself on this planet."

Dawn says, "I am sure you can, but this will limit your impact on the planet and reduce your visible footprint."

JD takes a pod down to the lower atmosphere and then dives off like an eagle over a rain forest. She is in her element and is visibly excited. She cries out in her native bird language with a joyful screech that echoes across the mountains. "Ops!" she says. "Well, that was an audio footprint, but not too damaging." She flies over a river looking at all the life. The multiple layers of life astound her.

JD speaks out loud, "This place has life on top of life on top of more life." She lands on a branch and takes samples. Then drops down to lower and lower levels taking more samples using the drone to package them in clear plastic containers. A snake jumps at her, but she catches it with twenty feather fingers from one wing holding it from head to tail. Her reflex and her vision are at a much higher level than the life around her. She holds the snake so it cannot move, studies it, able to see inside it, what it has eaten, and its biochemistry. She looks into its brain and thoughts. Then tosses it to a branch and studies how it lands. Bugs try to land on her, but her feathers automatically brush them away. The drone also blocks bugs and pollen from reaching her. She remarks out loud in English, “This is amazing!”.

Let's Meet For Drinks

The aliens study human communication and find a significant disconnect between the thoughts in brain waves and actual speech. The correlation between the two is highest in casual settings involving alcohol. So, they sent out an invitation for a casual meeting with drinks.

Leaders are in talks with their staff and then have the invitation appear in their minds. They appear distracted and then tell everyone to stop talking.

A leader from China speaks with a puzzled look, "I am listening to them. They just invited me for a drink. They don't like the word cocktail and say, "Is this a bird reference?" The next meeting is tomorrow. They don't give us much time to prepare, but I don't know how we can prepare anyway. I guess we won't have to worry about transportation as usual. I never know how to dress!"

The New Russian Leader

The new Russian leader Korlinkoff is ready for his first visit to meet the aliens and has heard about the transportation experience. He is going to work but is expecting a trip to visit the aliens. He looks at the surroundings checking to see if there is anything unusual. He asks his driver, "Driver, what is your name and where are you really taking me?" Driver says, "Sergey, and I am taking you to the Kremlin office as usual." Sergey thinks his leader is scared due to the demise of his predecessor.

Korlinkoff appears at work. He looks around, puzzled. Staff say hello and salute, but Korlinkoff looks at them for signs. He is acting strange. In the office, he still isn't sure this is real. Then, after work, on the way home, he starts to relax and falls asleep in the back seat of his limo.

He awakes in a cocktail gathering with the other leaders. At first, he thinks he is dreaming. An alien voice speaks directly to him. "You are not dreaming and you need to be alert."

All the other leaders are present. Beautiful bird pictures in their natural settings are on the wall and feathers in the drinks. The sign says, 'Authentic Cocktail drinks'. They have a sense of humor.

As they muddle about, half greeting each other, a bartender asks them what they would like. The bird man Sam appears, "Ladies and gentlemen, please all take a drink. I insist."

They all move to the bar, and their drinks are ready without asking, each getting what they were thinking about.

Sam states, "I thought we would just have some casual talk so I can get to know you better. Each of you has an assigned stand-up hover table; please proceed to your table so we can talk".

They each seem to know which table is theirs. When they arrive, Sam is there to meet each of them simultaneously. Again, messing with their perception of time.

Sam speaks to each of them simultaneously to save time. Questions come rapidly to prevent filtration of their thoughts and to better understand humans. "Hello, how are you today? What is your stress level 1-10; last night, this morning, and now? Before I arrived, what were the top issues you were working on? How is your leadership team working, how long have you known each other, and how many members in your family? Are they all well, safe, and going through what kind of challenges? What is snow made of? Where on Earth could you survive on your own? How many types of trees do you know? What is your net worth? What is your future plan for your children's children? Where is your species heading? What is your understanding of infinity?"

Questions come quickly, overlapping their responses. Their minds are challenged to keep up, words lag their thoughts, then no words are coming out, just thoughts, any ability to filter responses vanishes, then the questions blur, and their minds are racing, getting warm, its hot in here, cool air comes down on them, they start to get dizzy, then questions tail off.

Sam gives them a break, "Have another drink".

The drink has an unusually calming effect. They feel very happy now, content, and without worries. The bird man says "No worries, mate, be happy," followed by the song being played on invisible speakers, Sam disappears. Now they all go to the bar, look at each other, and try to talk but are too mentally fatigued. They walk out of the bar to their limos, but as they enter, they appear in their beds and fall asleep.

Sam is back in the spaceship, analyzing the responses. Character profiles appear in detail about their work, family, history, issues, work level, and stress patterns. Leaders are measured versus each other and the average population. Computer results start to filter out what makes them leaders and how each differs.

Back on the alien spaceship, Sam is on a round beam and starts spinning around it, holding on with his feet. He is in deep thought as he is fed information. His wife joins him and is taking the analysis to a higher level and sending the results to their home planets for review.

Elizabeth's Second Dream

Elizabeth is dreaming that she is walking out to her Ph.D. dissertation. But the university campus has changed, now more advanced, high tech. People in lab coats are running around in haste. She walks in but is now in a seating room around a large lab. It is an operating room. Several surgeons are operating on a large mass covered by a sheet. Surgeons pick up a large diamond from a stainless-steel tray. Then a large, gruesome hand appears. They saw open the skin with a rotary cutting blade and peel back the skin holding it in place with brackets. Dark red blood oozes out but then stops. They place the diamond on the knuckle of a hand that is still twitching. Her eyes turn towards the subject, and just as the face is about to appear, she wakes up suddenly and sits up in her bed. Confused, she wonders where this dream came from. Self-analyzing herself, she asks, "What events led me to this strange dream? This must be my initial trepidation from waiting to complete my Ph.D."

Inter Alien Negotiation for Planet Earth

The most advanced alien family meets with the first two alien ship leaders that are making a pitch as to why they should take over Earth.

Alien1: 820 level – the first to appear. Sam states, "Present your case for inhabiting Earth."

Alien 1 speaks, "We will allow human life to continue on this planet and will cleanse it of those with the disease. We will select 10% of the strongest with environmental re-engineering potential and recondition them back on our planet. Then return them to Earth to train the others. Those with cancerous tendencies that cannot be reconditioned with be contained or eliminated. Our technology will purge Earth of pollution over the next 200 years, restoring it to prehuman levels".

Sam to the second species, "Okay, now provide your proposal."

Alien 2 – 790 Level speaks, "Humans have brought nothing but destruction to this pearl. We have seen no evidence that they will preserve this miracle creation. This planet is self-cleaning, daily with gentle rains, flowing rivers, salted oceans, warm winds, freezing and thawing, radiation protection, magnetic poles... the list goes on. Who created such a masterpiece? Yet with all these gifts, humans, to use their own analogy, treat this like a Frat house party. They act like rock stars destroying the place for fun! It is time for Dad to come home and teach them a lesson they will not forget. They treat their cancers by surgery, chemistry, or radiation. We would treat human cancer the same and not allow another century of destruction. If you insist, 10% of the best could be maintained in balance with other species, but I don't recommend this as the cancer can reoccur. We understand your desire for diversification in this universe, but this is one cancer we should not preserve."

Alien 1000 Sam explains, "Points well understood. We will continue to assess all aspects and provides humans with time to respond and change. Also, let us see how hard they will battle to retain what they have. Then decide."

Discussion With the UN Leader of Earth

UN Leader speaks to Sam one on one in a requested meeting. “As I see it, we should be very happy you are here. You basically have our lives in your hand, and we are lucky that you are here to save us.”

Sam says, “I didn’t say that I will save your kind. Only give you the opportunity to save yourselves.”

Leader asks, “What would happen if you were to leave?”

Sam replies, “Some alien species would try to recondition a select group of humans, others would test humans as to their ability to withstand various means of elimination. Then having full knowledge of your kind, use the best methods to cleanse the planet.”

Leader asks, “They would torture us?”

Sam replies, “The word torture implies punishment to extract information and inflicting harm with no scientific purpose. They would be conducting scientific research without creating unnecessary pain. However, the testing would be fatal, followed by mass eliminations.”

Leader says, “That doesn’t sound appealing.”

Sam says, “Not to your species. Then they would bioengineer a change to adapt the planet’s atmosphere, vegetation, and food sources to allow their species to merge, including testing how their plant and animal species would intermingle with the existing ones. Keeping some species, eliminating those that are harmful. Earth would become a very different place, but free of your created pollution and threats."

Pause...

Sam continues, "Your next question is, "Can we just block out all alien species and let humans survive as is? If I were to hold back all invaders, you would still face your greatest risk."

UN Leader replies, "What is that?"

Sam states, "This you should know by now. Your species has suicidal tendencies. There is an alarming amount of this in your youth and at all ages, but I refer to the species on mass, long-term… I have a question for you. We have researched your financial evaluations but have found nothing on prewar scenarios. Our evaluation of multiple scenarios showed that outcomes of war are always at significant losses for both sides, financially and economically. Rarely do we ever see monetization of the environmental impact, loss of humans, long-term suffering, impact on the psyche of your children and long-term direction of humanity? Economic studies have a macro side but still nothing. Financial studies are micro tools only. A full analysis would place paramount effort on negotiating a solution. Yet negotiations studies are not a university degree or even a required course at any age. Our youth have years of studies on negotiation and evaluation of long-term impacts on our planet and our species rate and direction of development. My question, are pre-war scenarios completed in secret, not documented, or not done at all?"

UN Leader replies, "It is true that we do not have negotiation/resolution teaching as fundamental to our education. Most negotiation is on commercial terms to define pricing. We have trained along these lines. Your species is far more advanced, refined, and intellectual about the whole impact on your planet. We have a saying that might is right, and absolute power corrupts absolutely. Leaders who start wars do not conduct the kind of rigorous analysis that you expect. They are driven by ego, power, and the ability to seize an opportunity to expand their empires. This is how it was in our past and remains a threat today. However, this is diminishing with the advancement of our species. If you can share your training, I would propose this be added to our education system and make it a requirement for holding positions of power."

Transition Meeting With All Leaders and Their Staff

Sam is now in front of a large group of leaders at the UN and provides the results of his analysis, "We have conducted an analysis of your history via internet, books, your minds, interviewed your leaders and have tapped into the world's populations. There are significant challenges to the balance between humans, Earth and all other species. As we have done on other planets in similar situations, we give you an opportunity to prove yourselves. Your history shows a willingness to battle, and these battles bring out your best, and drive change and technology. To avoid destruction on a large scale, we propose battles one on one versus the alien races vying for your planet. This will accomplish several things: challenge you to advance the human species, utilize the best bioresources on your planet, bring a common purpose to all nations, and provide insight on other planets and species." He continues, "Given the vast differences in life forms and environments, we create a simulated battleground mid-way between the two home planets. To ensure interest, your Earth's continents will be wagered. Humans like to bet. If you lose, an alien species will move in and humans will move out. Note that, without our intervention, your species would be eliminated. The contestants must be 100% biological, no robotics or computer implants allowed. Take time to digest this challenge. Huston will provide further details." Sam turns to leave; no questions are raised as the leaders' minds are in shock.

Then as the leaders get up to leave, some are quick to respond to the challenge, "We need to assemble the best minds on battle strategy, training, biological enhancements, doctors, and on a world level."

Battle Rules

Huston is in charge of the battles and describes the rules in a broadcast from his spaceship as he sits in front of his battle room where scenes of past battles play. Planets of various types decorate the room in 3D holograms that come and go. In front of him is a control panel that allows him to modify battlegrounds. He connects to all the broadcasts throughout the Earth and begins to speak.

"Hello, future contestants and support groups. Here are some scenes from previous battles." The holographic images in his control room are shown to wide-eyed humans on Earth. Battle scenes on various planets emerge in strange forms never before seen by humans.

Huston continues, "Some battles last minutes, others, days. There may be the need to find water and even food. Some species hide out and wait for you to die from the elements or until you show yourself. Others are very aggressive and act fast. You can pick from offense to defense depending on your surroundings and your ability to adapt. No weapons are allowed; all must be contained within the living organism and based on elements from the home planet. The organism must be capable of living a minimum of 75% of its normal life span. Both contestants are in an unfamiliar environment, picked to be halfway between each native climate. Artificial breathing apparatus will be provided as necessary. Haste can be effective or lead to strategic mistakes, overexertion, injury from falls and hostile materials. You may even be battling against what you would consider being a plant or a series of connected plant creatures. A loss is determined by either death or an obvious permanent control by the other species. Mind control is one example, but this can only occur by physical intrusion into the body of the other species."

Scene of the planets where the competitor species comes from are displayed across Earth. Some have dust devils of huge tornados, and rains come down like spears, creating the need to run for shelter or carry shields. Others have scenes of constant volcanoes of lava spurting up hot acid. Some species live in advanced caves of rock and venture above ground only when weather permits, once every ten days. Gas planets species are like ghosts floating around eating small creatures that float on by. Buildings and homes are more solid forms of the gas that maintain their forms. Creatures can move in and out through the gas forms.

"As you can see from these few examples, the species you are up against have very different environments, harsh from your perspective. Harsh environments can lead to the more rapid development of their intellect and respect for their planets." Then he simply says, "Be prepared!"

Scientist Lab Scene

Bengal tigers, alligators, eagles and falcons, lizards, bats, chameleons, and snakes, are all placed in their elements and tested. Samples of skins, muscles, and brain cells are taken from everything from cats to ants. These samples are merged into human DNA.

Elizabeth Works With H33

Elizabeth, now 38, maintains a girlish charm with the intellectual look of a psychiatrist.

She is shown in a modern room with the walls displaying a 3D scene of beautiful landscapes, clean air, and birds. She watches the news which appears on the walls, moving to wherever she looks, and the landscapes are overwritten. News shows leaders with different views, minor conflicts, accidents, and pollution issues are becoming severe with new forms of pollution arising from chemical reactions between the many pollutants.

She turns it all off, walls turn into windows and the pollution outside is a stark contrast to her artificial screens. She exits through a wall that simply opens and she drops down to the ground level in an elevator that is only a blast of airflow that lets her down slowly.

She walks through a high-tech park towards a modern complex newly constructed and vast. Elizabeth, now with her Ph.D., is employed in the 'Enhancement Community' or EC. She comes in to assess the progress and speaks with the medical engineers on the status of the latest developments to be utilized on human combatants. She takes notes on items that affect their nervous system and psyche.

She calls her contender and future prospect combatant. "Hello, I am about to go into the operating room. Are you on the table yet?"

He responds with a very low growling tone, "Just walking in now."

"How do you feel after the secondary heart addition two days ago?" Elizabeth asks.

"Well, now I have two heartbeats," says the subject.

Elizabeth says, "So now you have more of a heart?"

"Very funny. Sorry, still heartless in that regard."

She enters the stadium-like complex, with multiple labs extracting organs from all sorts of animals and reptiles. Skin drafts, bat radar cells, ant brains, and muscle tissues are being merged with human cells. High-strength fibers are merged with muscle tissues. The nervous system is enhanced with a higher operating voltage for lightning-fast response.

She sits in a viewing room with a dozen other doctors and views the operation implanting the large pointed diamonds from a tray into his knuckles. She talks to the contender, "I guess this will be quick."

He responds, "Never quick enough. I cannot wait to use them."

The first diamond is implanted.

He asks, "How does it look?"

She says, “Deadly, with a brilliant shine.”

He says, “Excellent.”

She rubs a tear from the corner of one eye, thinking she should be accustomed to training combatants who fight to the death.

The head surgeon explains that he will be adding additional padding to reduce the shock to the bone. The bone has previously had enhanced toughness to prevent splintering under high impact. Anesthesia is never used, as each contender in training utilizes the experience to practice pain tolerance. The eyes of the otherwise covered patient look curiously at his hands, analyzing the work. No squinting from the pain.

As the skin is opened, bleeding begins, then the veins contract and the bleeding is halted. The skin has a shark-like texture, still human but thicker and tougher. The cutting causes some initial reflex reaction which is then controlled by the patient. Skin glue is used to close the cuts, UV light is then added to cure. The hands are then dipped in a viscous cloudy liquid. The surgeon exclaims, “Finished now! Everyone step back. Step BACK, I say.”

A warning light flashes. The 8-foot-high lethal fighter begins to rise, exposing the muscles of a Bengal tiger, massive skull, short blunt nose, wide neck almost to his shoulders, razor-sharp fingernails like daggers, feet with sharp bone surfaces, pointed kneecaps, protective armor skull of a rhino. His face shows highly developed intellect and quick eye movement. Fear is palpable in all the doctors and sweat starts to roll. The Rep in training knocks his fists together to hear the sharp twang, dampened by the thick skin. Then hits himself in the chin with a resounding thump. He is pleased; a smile breaks out.

Then he speaks, "NOW FOR THE TESTING!" And bolts out of the operating room, tearing the door off its hinges. "Jesus", cries out one doctor.

The other says, "Mother of God," a nurse grabs a table as she almost passes out. A sigh of relief breaks out in the room.

Training Room

The enhanced contender strides into the training room, twice the size of a football field, with all sorts of obstacles, including dummy alien creatures. He sprints in and is met by several trainer doctors in lab coats. The doors close behind him.

Battle Intel Training

Earth's Contenders are given training on potential alien species: how to ID vital organs, how they may be protected by hardcovers, how to look for penetration points for max impact, and back door entrances to strike vital organs.

Training is given to assess the environment of the battle site: gravity, viscosity, the density of the atmosphere, density underfoot, the ability to push off to generate power, winds, waves, radiation, and toxicity. In battle, the effect of all of these factors on your strength, endurance and mental state must be considered.

Contender enhancements include brain cell injections from ant brains into the small voids of the brain. IQ is increased by 65%. Enhanced interconnectivity between nerve synapses drives up the brain's clock speed and allows rapid access to muscles for lightning quick reflexes.

Muscle cell enhancements are made with Bengal tiger muscle cells enhanced with ant fibers to obtain ant-like strength to weight ratios.

Gym and Training

Contenders enter the massive training and testing stadium. There are massive boulders to push, lift or throw. Running and sprinting areas, up steep hills, rocky, loose terrain, underwater obstacle courses, trees and vines to climb, and animal fighting areas (rhinos, tigers, giant crocs, elephants, snakes). Many potential combatants are fighting animals underwater as well as above and exercising with massive objects.

The combatant now selected for the battle is called H33. He is leaving the gym, sweat steaming off him and he jumps into an ice-cold bath with the sound of lava hitting the water. His skin is glowing from the heat and now cools. Muscles are twitching from the rapid nerve synopsis. Probes monitor his temperature, cool, down rate, heart rate, brain processing speed and his new backup heart.

Serenity, his companion, comes to meet him as he is getting dressed to return. She smiles and makes comforting comments about his enhanced performance in the gym, adding that his dinner and massage await. Warm lights lead the way, opening up ahead in the hallways. Alarms sound to warn others. One overweight lab technician in deep thought does not heed the warning. He walks with his head down out of a doorway into H33, whose left arm reacts and sends the technician flying into the ceiling. H33 shakes his head but continues walking. He sees that the tech is okay but moaning in pain. Serenity looks back but then continues her soft conversation trying to relax H33.

They arrive at their quarters, which are surrounded by danger signs, “Keep out or face imminent death, Rep quarters are nearby.”

Night Time in Resting Quarters

Serenity guides H33 to his massage table custom made to his form. He lies on his back; the top half of the table drops down from the ceiling to encase him. The case then fills with pure oxygen. Vibrations occur with temperature cycles and light electrical shocks. After one hour, it opens and H33 walks into the dining room. He sits in his meal chair and intravenous food flows into each limb. He also has a tube to flowing nourishment into his stomach.

After that, he moves into his white bedroom with its heavily padded walls and floor. There is a raised platform that looks like a bed of thick green grass. He lies in it as it moves with his body. His mind drifts back to a time when he had a real room, but then he loses the thought with a flashback to a time when he had a violent dream, destroying his room and almost killing Serenity.

Flashback to the Early Days

Serenity was sitting next to Aran before he became H33. He is human with just a few mods. They are eating together in a regular home, but Aran is 7 ft tall and muscular, though not yet heavily enhanced. He drinks green-colored milkshakes and tears at nearly raw steaks with blood dripping down his chin. Serenity keeps bringing him nuts, fruits and vegetables. She gives him a deep massage using her elbows and knees and says, “Looking great! How do you feel?”

He responds, “Crazy strong and hyper, not sure I can sleep.”

Serenity, “Then take one of these.” He does and drifts to sleep but is contorting in his bed. She is on her own bed across the room and is watching him, taking notes.

Then suddenly, he gets up, sleep-walks, and breaks into a fight against an invisible creature. He breaks up the room and throws the bed. Serenity dives across the room, the door is broken and she manages to get out. She calls the lab “999 Rep out of control”. Within 30 seconds, 5 lab coats arrive and fire darts at him. He opens his eyes, sees them, moves to attack, then realizes he has had a dream, waits, the darts take effect, and he falls to the floor.

Meeting One on One with the US President

President of the USA has had a busy day that started at 7 AM. Now at 3:00, he sees he has an appointment in his calendar for 30 minutes.

He calls his secretary, "What is this appointment with Dr. Oiseaux?"

She says, "I don't recall making that."

He thinks, *damn, I know what it is.* The bird man Sam walks in with a smile, "Nice of you to take my appointment on such short notice!"

US President, "It's my pleasure, as you are my number one priority."

Sam, "Yes, I know you have a lot of priorities. Most of them start in this office. I am here to talk about a change. I need to understand your propensity to change, adapt, and understand a new way. Tell me about your past adaptations. When were you reluctant, and how did you succumb?" He starts to tell stories that blur out.

Sam, "What is your limitation to change? Personally, your staff, your people, the speed of change is governed by?"

Again, the conversation takes on a rapid pace. The US president seems to lose control as he races to provide the answers. Honest, deep replies come out directly to the alien.

He somehow realizes on the most basic level that he cannot tailor his responses. They come out raw and full bore at his mind's limit.

The president starts to regain control of his own consciousness. Sam says, "Thanks for your honest and in-depth response," but appears unsatisfied. Who has the highest capacity for change? The president mentions a young, brilliant woman in his cabinet.

"Where is she now?" asks Sam as he walks out.

Sam figures out who it is in the office. A sharply dressed, colorful lady with red hair is busy talking with someone next to her and typing at the same time. She looks up and drops the conversation and closes her computer. Their eyes meet, Sam analyzes her thoughts through her brain waves and picks up her name. "Lucille, do you have time for a chat?" she quickly realizes that this is Sam, and she bolts up from her chair, her skin tingling with excitement. She nods and gets up as they walk out.

Alien 1000 Computer Analysis of Humans on Earth

Dawn calls in the family, “Analysis from home has arrived.” They all gather in a large room, where a simulated tree forest of their home world dissolves and makes way for indiscernible groups of screens of colors and graphs that only their species can understand.

Dawn speaks to Sam, Huston and JD. “Before we view the results, we have seen children of different races playing together, sharing toys, helping each other. Yet when they grow old, something happens. They develop hatred and fight to gain more wealth and influence. Tracing the sources, education in their schools does not seem to be the issue. Media and other outside influences are in play. Competition in the workplace is one source. Forced living in high density is also a factor. Strange how this comes about. We have seen the reverse trend in most other advanced species.”

Dawn says, “Let me ask the children in the world to see if they have the answers.”

Dawn communicates directly with all the children of the world, “Would you like to play with other races?”

Children’s average response comes, generated by the computer in a child’s voice, “Yes, of course, especially if they like to play the same games as me.”

Dawn again directly, “Do your parents dislike people from other races?”

Children’s average response is, “Well, yes, they do not like them.”

Dawn, “Do you know why?”

Children, “No, but our government, press, and religious leaders do not like them either.”

Dawn is now just talking to her family, “Children here are influenced to dislike other races!”

Dawn says, “I have a question for all the leaders. Computer asks all adult humans in tier 1 and tier 2 leadership roles the following: Are humans destroying the Earth? Are the efforts in place sufficient to prevent this? If not, why not?”

The family realizes this will take some time, so they walk into the next room to sip some water from an ice blue water fountain that has a circular flow that spirals up and spills back over.

They return after several minutes.

Computer, “Results, 78% believe humans are destroying the Earth. 52% believe efforts are sufficient. 48% believe it will not happen in their lifetime. Therefore, avoid any short-term discomfort.”

Dawn says, “Computer, does Earth’s education process include multi-lifetime problem-solving?”

Computer's results moments later, "Long term business, engineering, and science problems forecast less than twenty years."

Dawn looks at the others in their family. They jointly realize the extent of the problem.

Dawn says, "Okay, let's see the results from home."

A voice from their home planet describes the outcome of the Earth's analysis, "The human species has a category 1 malignancy with their major drive to consume to excess, all things of pleasure. Reproduction rates show no sign of abatement. Potential to spread to other worlds if interstellar travel is developed before self-destruction."

Many scenarios flash by showing increased pollution, massive open pit mining, and deforestation. Attempts to restore balance are made by some countries while others go unchecked. Feudal battles continue at low levels. Conservation efforts are made but made too late. Humans launch spaceships to seed other planets.

"One simple solution is a calculated meteor strike at the center of the rotational gravity of the Earth, just below the equator. This will create sufficient debris to wipe out 90% of the population and move Earth's orbit out, reducing temperatures to original levels. Rotational speed would decrease to 31-hour days."

Dawn speaks, "This would be a repeat and could simply create another species incapable of managing this planet effectively. Computer, what about a pure garden planet with a level one non-intelligent species? Could this be a viable long-term solution?"

The computer speaks, "Solution possible with multiple meteorite strikes to eliminate all intelligent life. Insect varieties are key to plant growth, followed by small mammals to control insect levels. Sea life continues to gain intelligence and would transfer to land. In 1.5 billion years, intelligent life would return. Suggest a higher percentage of the sea surface to 80%. This would reduce the polluting capacity of land-based species, postponing pollution buildup to current levels by 1.5 billion years."

Sam says, "Yes, we see numerous options along these lines. However, the planet loses its biodiversity and becomes nearly inert for half a billion years. First, I would attempt to retrain the existing species to see if they could become self-aware of their cancerous traits. They have sufficient intelligence to advance themselves. Their survival instincts need to be triggered. This has been a necessity in their primitive development, but the richness of the planet has made them soft and thirsty for pleasure."

Dawn speaks, "The implementation plan needs to educate their youth to avoid cancerous tendencies; develop skills to isolate the activities that destroy their host and eventually themselves with no purpose other than excessive consumption."

JD says, "Have any of you seen signs of an alien injection into this planet that has caused humans to be out of sync with their planet? There was an evolution discontinuity between apes and man."

Dawn says, "Computer, has there been an alien injection into the human race?"

Computing… "Earth shows signs of 80% natural development and 20% foreign element."

Dawn asks, "What is the source of the foreign element?"

The computer speaks, "Meteorites, gamma ray strikes, solar radiation and evidence of other unknown elements or interactions."

Sam replies, "Yes, we have seen this unknown element before. Something unusual has happened here. We have seen clues of foreign elements, but the originating sources have vanished. If only we could tell how traces have been eliminated."

Huston steps in, hearing the conversation with the computer. "Did you see the period when the Earth was ruled by dinosaurs?"

Sam says, "Yes, it was interesting but relevant?"

“They were all wiped out by a surgical meteorite strike similar to the number one option,” says Huston. “Dad, were you here before?” he asks jokingly.

Sam says, “Computer, compare your meteorite strike calculations with the impact off the coast of Mexico that ended the dinosaur period.”

The computer says, “83% similarity.”

Huston, now more excited that he has hit on something, “Wow, Computer, did our species do this? Any record of our visit to this area?”

The computer replies, “No records of this in our system, but this predates our intervention protocols.”

Sam asks, “Computer, what is the possibility of that meteorite strike being directed by an alien species versus it being a natural event?”

The computer replies, “Meteorite strikes were frequent in that era, given the evidence of impact craters on Earth and the moon. Of that size, rare. Precisely that size to wipe out a species but maintain other forms of life, estimated at 0.1%. Probability of a species in this region desiring and capable of implementing this is 0.01%. Evidence of an Alien intervention, none.”

Huston asks, “Dad, where were you in this period? Mom, what was Dad’s interstellar reputation like in those days?”

Dawn replies, “He was wondering the universe aimlessly before he met me.”

They all smile and laugh.

Sam says, “Computer, clear this record as this is but a joke.”

The computer speaks, “I don’t record jokes below a rating of 4 or below, so it has been erased.”

Huston says, “Hey, it was better than that.”

Sam says, “Computers never lie, Son.”

H11 Blue Snow Blizzard Battle

H11 appears next to Huston in a holding zone, looking onto an alien planet. H11 was selected from the first 10 prospective combatants. His agility, strength and cunning put him ahead of the others. Combatants are developed in groups of 10. The selected one from the first batch is called H11.

Huston says, "You will need this eye protection plus this suit and snowshoes but note this is not snow as you know it. I will give you the same advice I gave the other species. Watch your footing and good luck."

H11 puts them on and moves toward the fluid door, and gives a thumbs up, knowing they are watching back on Earth.

He enters a blue landscape with a green sky, but everything looks upside down. The wind is howling, mountains of blue snow move like waves on an ocean, but slow and viscous. He can walk on it but sinks to his knees even with the snowshoes.

A big wave of snow comes. He will get swept away and buried if he cannot ride it. He dives to body surf, but he is rolled several times and ends upside down with his snowshoes on the surface. He battles to the right of himself and sees another coming. This time he crouches down to a surfing position and tries to ski down the wave, wipes out but swims back to the surface. He thinks – will the combatant come from above or from below the surface or on a wave? He is stumbling off balance but tries to get ready for an attack. He tries to walk; then running fast works and he moves up a mountain side that is more solid. He climbs to a firm area and stops on a ledge. He completes a survey for signs of life. Airborne life is possible, wind shear is moderate, and shifting ground is dangerous for life. Underground is possibly more stable for life. No signs of any food sources. Above the blue waves, it is green, but not an atmosphere that thins out. Eyesight may not be calibrated for this planet.

Then he sees a trail on the snow. Is it wind or something else? There are three parallel lines heading towards me. This is a threat, and his heart rate rises to the initial combat level. I have a solid ground and elevation advantage. Need to maintain solid ground contact for power. Will try to take the creature in hand and maintain control and use my lower body weapons. A movement towards him stops 160 meters away. Trails disappear in the wind. A large wave moves towards that spot. He loses his position. He gets hit with a massive snowball that knocks him off his ledge and he tumbles down the mountainside in an avalanche. He is able to get on top of the snow and hits a 4-point ski stance on his knees and forearms. He sees the green creature skiing towards him as he is now skiing away. It is an expert in these conditions. An attack from his back will put him at a great disadvantage. The creature is catching up and about to make contact. At the last minute, he flips and breaks with both snowshoes and points his arms at the low point of the creature. It tries to jump over him, but he reaches up to catch one of its three legs and shears it off. It bleeds green, then freezes and stops. Placed in the snow, it starts to mend. H11 sees he has the advantage and attacks it head-on. They tumble in the snow together. It has tentacles that come out of its head. He grabs it by the throat, but a tentacle pierces the back of his skull into his spine. It now controls his body. His arms and legs go limp. Then it sends nerve signals to stop his main heart, then his other heart.

Hawaii Is Lost To the Alien Race – Human Evacuation after the First Loss

Sam makes a joint announcement with the Earth leaders; Hawaii has been lost. All humans had watched the broadcasted battle. They know that this is better than total annihilation, yet they still cry. Some refuse to leave their homes in Hawaii. The aliens step in and use a beam of energy to calm them and provide a permanent perspective of the situation. Then they leave Hawaii on their own. They say, "We will win it back one day and at least we still have another home. Hopefully, our new guests don't change it too much."

Ships take people and their belongings to their new homes where the others welcome them and try to make them comfortable, knowing that they may also be in the same situation soon.

In Hawaii, one week later, streets are empty, lights are out, and wildlife enters the cities. Then new aliens start to appear, analyzing the building materials and how they can ecologically recycle them. In fields, they plant their own strange crops in small samples to view their interaction with the soil and air. They purify drinking water. Humans can view this via satellite pictures.

The new aliens love Hawaii. They are in heaven as they swim in the surf, play with the fish, communicate with the dolphins, developing a friendship. They take down the shipping docks and oil supply containers and use the materials to build homes high in the mountains away from potential tidal waves but also construct day homes near the beach. They start planting fruits from their home planet and grow algae along the shore, using the strong currents to accelerate growth.

Aliens lie on the shores, sunning themselves and playing with their families like they are on vacation and confident they have the situation in hand.

In the evening, after a hard day's work, they meditate on sunset and thank the universe for this gift and their chance to enjoy it. They pray to say thank you to the universe for this beautiful moment in time, and yes, we appreciate that this is but a brief transient gift that will become something even more beautiful in the future.

Humans, contenders, scientists, and leaders are motivated by this loss and shake their hands, pound their fists, swearing to win the next battle.

Eye In The Back Of the Head

Medical and tactical combat analysts review the tape of the loss. The key moment was when H11 was hit in the back of the head with a massive snowball that he did not see. Humans lack the 360-degree vision that aliens from other planets have. Current contenders have between 160 and 174 degrees of vision. Vision accuracy drops at angles above145 degrees to zero at 180 degrees.

A team of optical surgeons is assembled by the head of medical technologies, Dr. Brenner.

The top ten surgeons from around the world gather in the battle room. They have been on site working together for seven months.

Dr. Brenner addresses them, “Our battle was lost due to a lack of vision on the incoming projectile. Your task is to rectify the issue and provide a 360-degree vision. Suggestions? I remind you we don’t have much time.”

There is a pause. They know there is only one solution, but it seems too radical.

The German surgeon speaks with a thick accent, “We all know that we must drill a hole in the back of the head, enlarge the skull, implant a genetically compatible eye complete with its original nerve system and somehow link these nerve endings in parallel with the existing eye paths into the brain. Then we need to train the brain on how to process this new information, first by covering the existing eyes until the brain sees only at the back. Then opening the covers to the frontal signals. Confusion is likely at this point until therapy can rectify the images."

The other surgeons sit back and sigh at the enormity of the task.

The Norwegian surgeon speaks up, "This is very complex. Possible but unlikely that we will get this right the first time. We need several trials before we can be sure of success on a fighter."

A female surgeon from India said, "If you are looking for my expertise to grow an eye from embryo cells, then you are looking at over a year. The eye must be grown within a brain to develop the nerves required. We have yet to grow a brain. I suggest we look for a donor."

Dr. Brenner speaks, "A worldwide donor list has been created. We have mapped many DNA sequences from the world population and linked them to our combatants. I will initiate the search for an eye."

Indian surgeon says, "One other point. The nerve endings need to survive the transfer and have the ability to adapt to the new host. The age of the eye should be just as it reaches full size."

Dr. Brenner says, “Unless we are super lucky with an incident and the right DNA and age, we will have to find a volunteer. I will send out requests for volunteers that meet our requirements, sad as this may be. The rest of you get to work.”

Volunteers

Notices are electronically sent to the five homes on Earth where a match exists.

The first is a girl 11 years old and the mother reads the notice with the father in the room. She turns white and freezes. Father sees this, “Honey, what’s wrong?”

Mother says, “They want her eye!” and she starts to cry.

Father asks, “Whose eye? Who wants it?”

Mother replies, “Dr. Brenner wants Trisha’s eye.” (Everyone knows Dr. Brenner from the daily news on fighter developments).

Father replies, “What?” and he runs to check on his daughter in the next room. “How is your eyesight, honey?

Trisha is wearing a corrective eye covering. “It is getting better.”

Father says, “Your eyesight is shit. Don’t mislead anyone until it is perfect.”

Father turns to mother, “Nothing to worry about, dear. They don’t want her bad eyes.” He videotapes his daughter’s condition and sends it to Dr. Brenner.”

Family Two in China

In a remote village in the mountains of China lives a father, mother and a young boy. They live in a small, reclaimed brick home but with electricity and internet. A government official visits them with the news. "Your son Wulin is needed to provide for a combatant – to provide one of his eyes so that he can see backward."

Parents freeze and say no, but their ten years old son hears the request from just outside. At the back of the house, he was resoldering a computer board on a drone. The boy walks around to the front of the house and says, "I will do it. Just one eye? I can still see, and I will be famous, plus be part of a combatant for the world?"

The official responds, "Yes, and they will try to replace the eye. You will be very well treated."

The father says no and the mother cries no. The boy looks around at his poor surroundings but beautiful mountains. He goes to hug his father and mother, who hold on tight. He whispers to them, "I love you, but I am going to save the world and see the technology." Then ducks under their hugs and runs to the officer's vehicle and they speed off as the parents run after them.

Mountain Scene

Two humans are climbing up a blue ice mountain near Lake Louise. One is climbing alone up high above his friend on the blue ice. The alien Sam is sitting on top of the ledge, looking at the beautiful scenery.

The climber makes it to the top and sees the alien, but its light blue feathers match the crystal-clear blue ice. He shakes his head in disbelief. Then Sam speaks. He is startled but then realizes who this is from the news.

Sam speaks, "It is remarkable the textures that water makes on this planet. Truly unsurpassed in its beauty in the universe. Do you realize how fortunate you are to be here, climbing and enjoying this view? Crystal clear sky, except for the pollution on the horizon. Do you know how this snow is created?"

The climber takes a minute to respond as he is in shock at meeting the alien and doesn't know what to say. "Yeah, I love it here, one of the few places still untouched. Snow crystals are formed by water mixed with dust particles. The crystals grow with more water vapor as they fall. They continue to crystallize in the sun. Each day they become more rigid. These flows, here over this edge are melting glaciers that formed over centuries."

Sam plays back in his head the response from leaders that had no idea how the snow was formed and did not care. Sam waves a wing and feather fingers to him in a half-bowing motion. "It was a pleasure to watch you succeed in your climb. Don't take this beauty for granted," and he flies off.

Meanwhile, his climbing partner makes it to the top and sees the bird alien fly off and says, "Wow, is that who I think it is?"

"Yeah."

"What did he do or say?"

"He was just watching us climb, asked me how snow is made and said this was the most beautiful place in the universe."

"Didn't you ask him anything?"

Climber #1 says, "Man, I could hardly speak, thought I imagined it. He blended in with the ice like camouflage. I thought I was talking to a ghost until you said you saw him."

H22 Bad Rain Battle

Huston is speaking to H22. "I hope you learned from H11's experience. The planet's atmosphere is not that different from yours. Good luck. No special apparatus required."

H22 observes the planet and believes it is self-destructing. Rain is either piercing bullets or large chunks the size of irregular bricks. He must find shelter fast. Finds something resembling a palm tree with strong fibers resistant to the rain bullets. Under this, he is safe. Then he sees rain runoff from the mountains coming like an avalanche of boulders. He climbs inside the tip of the V of the palm tree. The tree is hit by the avalanche but then flips to a Y, and he is on top, floating down the boulder avalanche. The rain bricks are hitting him. He is getting beat up. He sees a large flat rock floating nearby. Cannot reach it without falling into the boulder river. Sees another, it comes close. He picks it up, but this action almost tips his tree boat over. He lies on his back with his knees on his chest and the rock shield on top of him. He is floating down the river fast and looking at the side banks that are moving more slowly. Some clip on his side and he starts to bleed. The dagger rain slows to small bullets then stops. The river slows, and he approaches the less moving banks and jumps off.

The boulder bank moves under his feet and he has to catch his balance. He keeps jumping further away from the moving river until the ground is a stationary pile of boulders.

He sits and looks at all the cuts and bruises he has suffered. Then looks around at his surroundings. Not a pretty sight of shifting rock and a black sky. The storm is passing away, leaving a dark trail of rain. More storms in the distance are coming his way. Looking for his fellow combatant, he would prefer to have the fight now before the next storm injures or kills him. The oncoming storms look like hurricanes compared to the rain shower he just experienced. Where is the other contestant? He screams out loud, trying to get it to hear him.

Could this be simply, who can survive the longest? There is nothing that resembles food or water on this planet. But where does the rain come from? How do these rocks evaporate and become rain? The volcanic activity must be the cause. Cannot see far, given the black sky storms. The palm-like tree made of a Kevlar-like fiber must come from a forest nearby. He must move back upriver. He begins to run, looking at incoming storms to try to avoid them. They move very slowly, so this may be possible. He stumbles between the boulders. His leg gets caught and almost breaks. Badly bruised, he continues, looking around for his combatant. Then he sees a boulder coming at him with speed. He tries to avoid it, but with his injured leg, it hits him as he falls away. The impact was not very damaging, but he falls in between the boulders and is stuck. A large sand-colored creature appears with a massive boulder in its hand and crushes his skull.

Australia is Lost

Humans watch live videos as the aliens move in after a full evacuation of Australia. Kangaroos watch the aliens, and after seeing the strange creatures, pause, confused, then run. The aliens are humanoid with sand-colored skin, no hair and have an eye band that stretches 60% of the way around their heads. They have one hearing organ that protrudes from the top of their head-like, a small satellite receiver. It moves from right to left as it picks up sounds and flattens down to the head if threatened.

These aliens love the deserts of Australia and feel at home on the dry lands, venturing into the coasts to begin to grow their crops, planting seeds from their home world. They are slender 9 feet tall and can run at high speeds with the two joints in their legs that provide whip-like movement.

Human Leaders Unite and Discuss Drastic Options

The newly elected world UN leader Lucille speaks, "If we don't start winning the alien battles, we will lose the planet. If we don't take drastic measures to preserve the planet, we will lose the planet. Our species is very near extinction. We must act now and look at all the options. I don't want to hear that any of these are too drastic or inhumane. We are here to rank them in order of implementation. Our best scientists will now present the options."

Scientist from China says, "The root cause and the elephant in the room for too long is population growth. We enforced a one-child policy in the past. We must now have a zero-child policy. We have just implemented this with little backlash in China. The rest of the world must follow suit. Laws must be enacted tomorrow. Birth control drugs need to be added to the water systems."

Lucille speaks, "Does anyone disagree?" The USA agrees Russia agrees, United Europe agrees, SA, Africa, and Australasia all agree.

"Okay, inform your countries now." They all speak to their cabinets back home and the rulings are put in place. "Those already pregnant?"

A pause – a leader speaks up, "We are not murderers. All abortions are legal but not required by law."

Lucille continues, "Use of any oil/gas burning devise including cars, trucks, industry, electricity generation to be prohibited worldwide. All agree? Good – notify your homelands." They send the message. It is done.

"Wood burning prohibited." All agree and state 'done' as they communicate back home.

"Workers reassigned to environmental cleanup. Each country to move 50% of its workforce to environmental clean-up." Each item tabled is automatically agreed to and orders are sent back home.

"Green space increase. Any space that can be reassigned to plant life must be. No pesticides. Weeds are our friends as they consume CO2. In the home and in the yard, plant the species that grow fastest and eat up the most C02. Guidelines have been created and need to be enforced at the city level."

"Do we have 100% agreement?" from the UN leader Lucille. Yes, yes, and yes, sound around the room.

"Some of you are silent. I suggest we wage war on any nation that does not participate 100%. We will make a joint announcement to the world tomorrow at 12:00 GMT. Also, any rioting? Police will shoot to kill. Note we have excess population." UN leader has now become very aggressive with a marked change in personality.

The Eye Implant

Wulin is escorted into the hospital and prepared for surgery. He is on a stretcher going into the operating room. The combatant is already there. It is H33 and he hears the boy coming in. He is on his stomach with his head shaved, ready for drilling.

"Hello, Wulin," says H33 in his softest voice that is still startling and rumbles like distant thunder.

Wulin is startled and excited to see H33's size and grotesque figure. He looks at his many implants and says, "Cool."

H33 continues, "You are a very brave boy and I thank you for your precious gift." I will fight even harder now to preserve it and your future."

Wulin swallows hard to speak, "I think you are the bravest in fights to the death. For me, it is just one eye."

H33 scans Wulin with his senses, and by the rapid light heartbeat, the tone of his voice, his size (using his radar and even his smell), he guesses his age. "What? you must be around 10 years old."

Wulin says, "Yes, sir, H33."

H33 now in a loud booming voice, "Doc, 10 years old, what the hell!"

Dr. Brenner, who is supervising the operation, speaks up, “Yes, unfortunately, old eyes will not be successful as they will not adapt to a new host.”

H33 speaks, “Dam, the price is always high. Wulin, take my hand”. Wulin reaches next to him to grab his hand, but it is ten times bigger than his, so he just grabs a finger.

H33 says, “We can go to sleep now (he senses the operation is about to begin as everyone has stopped moving around the room). Can you count to ten for me in your language so I can learn?”

Wulin starts to count, “Yī' èr sān,” but at 3, he falls asleep.

H33 says, “Poor kid. So brave and generous.” His eyes water, and he lays on his stomach, looking at the floor. A tear drops down in front of him. He watches it lie there, then he falls asleep too.

Drilling begins with the sound of flesh and bone tearing. A team of surgeons works on the boy and on H33 simultaneously. Neurological networks appear on large screens over each patient. The maps are a complex network of electrical pathways showing microvolt signal strengths. They focus on the boy’s eye network and the connections to his brain. The head surgeon speaks, “We must take the eye, optic nerve up to the optic chiasm and the lateral geniculate nucleus to provide the 3rd signal to the primary visual cortex of H33."

H33 brain's cavity is cut open, exposing the back of his brain. Inside the optical section of the brain is seen with the nerve network.

The surgeon says, "With the primary visual cortex of the brain at the back of the head, the installation is actually less invasive, but space is short. Hence we enlarge the skull and have a straight line from the eye to the brain."

The boy's eye system is installed using a combination of robotics and the surgeon's gloved hands. The surgeon is sweating and the nurse clears the sweat from his forehead every few minutes. After three hours, the surgeon pulls back, completing his work.

"We will need to draw a signal from the new eye to make the connection," says the head surgeon. He flashes a light into the newly installed eye and sends an activating signal to H33's brain receptors. The nerve systems show a link to the brain. "Installation complete," he proclaims. "Now we add stem cells and previously drawn fluids to heal the brain quickly." H33 is closed up with rhino skull plaster to make his skull stronger than before.

The focus was all on H33 while the second team's surgeon installed Wulin's new glass eye. Now they patch him up and place a large bandage over his eye. He is rolled out to the normal hospital recovery room. H33 is returned to the research lab for his special treatment.

Recovery

After three days of recovery, H33's eye covering is about to be removed. Surgeons and optical physiotherapists await.

The head surgeon removes the bandages and takes a look. The eye is small and sunken into the skull, well protected. The brown eye matches his brown skin and hair. "H33, your new eye has healed nicely. Don't expect to see a clear 360-degree image. Your brain will have to learn to process the new information."

H33 speaks, "Wow, I can see everything 360 degrees like I am outside my own body!"

The crowd jumps with excitement.

The surgeon is skeptical, "Really, you can see through it?"

H33 says, "No, not a damn thing. I was just joking. When do you turn it on?"

The surgeon says, "As expected, we need to train your brain. And not just so it doesn't tell jokes! But also to see with the third eye. We are going to put this blindfold over your original eyes. Then your brain will be forced to use the new one."

H33 says, "Great, so I have to walk backward now?"

The Surgeon says, "It wouldn't hurt."

They put on the blindfold and wait…

H33 says, "It's not working. Did you install the switch?"

The Surgeon asks, "Is it dark or light?"

H33 replies, "Cloudy with dark patches."

The Surgeon says, "Here I will flash a light," and he points a flashlight at his eye.

H33 jumps, "You don't have to stick it in my eye!"

The Surgeon says, "Good, you have a solid link. Therapy can begin. Practice walking backward."

H33 asks, "How is Wulin doing?"

The Surgeon replies, "The other team is handling that; they will let you know when they are finished."

Wulin's Operation

Wulin has remained unconscious for several hours in the recovery room. When he awakes, a nurse is by his side. She asks, "Wulin, how do you feel?"

Wulin tries to speak but mumbles. Then words come out, "Headache, bad."

The nurse calls in the surgeon who patched up Wulin. He arrives a few minutes later.

Surgeon 2 enters, "Hello, how is he?"

The nurse replies, "Trouble speaking and has a bad headache."

The surgeon looks into his good eye, which has no movement. He takes a light and flashes it. Still no movement.

"Wulin, can you see the light?"

Wulin says, "No, it's too dark."

Surgeon two takes the nurse aside, "The focus was on ensuring H33's implant was a success and a large section of optical nerves and surrounding tissue was taken. His condition is not a complete surprise."

The nurse asks, "So he is blind in both eyes? You will operate to solve this?"

Surgeon 2 says, "I will get a team to look at the options. They took out his main optical network and surrounded his brain cells. I hope I can get some action, but given the circumstances, other priorities…"

The Nurse says, "Unbelievable!" and walks away and holds Wulin's hand and tells him, "Don't worry, Wulin, I will take good care of you and you will get better."

Dawn has been watching the operation via the fly like probes that she had sent into the operating room and throughout the hospital. She is affected by what she sees and decides to step in. She flies to the hospital in a small spacecraft with bird-like wings that change shape with speed. She lands next to the hospital emergency entrance with the small vehicle, gets out and walks in. The guards see her and step aside. She knows exactly where to go to find Wulin. The nurse is there holding his hand.

Dawn says, "I can't stand this, so I will correct Wulin's eyesight and bring him back to his family. Will you help bring him to my ship?"

The nurse says, "Thank god, yes. And YES," she says, very happy and with a fist pump. "Wulin, your eyesight will be corrected by the aliens now. Everything will be okay and you will be returned to your family."

Wulin is in a daze and doesn't understand, "Aliens? Here?"

He is pushed by the nurse to follow Dawn down the hallways. Everyone just steps aside and stares.

The guard at the door is puzzled, seeing Wulin moving with the nurse and alien. Nurse says to the guard, "Dawn will take Wulin, who lost his eyesight to H33 and she will fix him."

The guard replies, "Okay good, need help?"

Dawn waves a few feather fingers, and the door to the vehicle opens and a soft white board slides out. They place Wulin on the board, it retracts. The doors close and Dawn steps in. There is a gust of air pulling the ship forward as flexible white wings pull out. The wings become large with camber, but as the ship gains speed, they retract smaller and smaller. Air is channeled through tubes built into its surface and accelerated for propulsion. The ship circles upward and is gone.

Onboard the Alien Ship With Wulin

Wulin had been so excited to contribute to the cause, but after the operation, his mind was not the same, and without his vision, he lived in a dream. Despair was short lived, as he tried to replace it with his everyday calm. Dark thoughts would come and go.

Dawn spoke to him, “Wulin, I saw what you offered. This was no small gift. I cannot let this brave and selfless act be punished like this. You will go through a small painless process, and afterward, you will be better than before.

Wulin’s board holding him floats into a large operating room. The board disappears along with his clothes. He is floating in a large room filled with tools of different shapes and textures. Some are silver and metallic looking. Others are soft and flexible. Straps come out and hold him by his ankles and wrists. Others circle his neck, head and waist. They begin to analyze his body functions. An intravenous tube enters each arm and leg. Blood flows into a cube that analyzes it. On the large 3D holographic screen, each of his organs are analyzed for function. Some minor abnormalities are seen and corrected.

Wulin mumbles, but Dawn reads his thoughts, “I feel funny like I am being tickled from the inside.”

Dawn says, “Very good, that is exactly what is happening. It is better that we keep you awake during the procedure. Let me know what else you feel later.”

The computer screen stops analysis and starts programing the operation. The brain is now zoomed in on and the severed nerve endings and brain damage enlarged. The source of the blindness is discovered, and the list of procedures required to repair dance on the screen in bird language with letters looking like feathers.

After several minutes, the summary of the operation is displayed. Eye vision to be restored to human levels plus 20% improved resolution. Wulin’s near sightedness to be corrected along with his astigmatism.

Brain damage requires the growth of new brain cells. Nerve endings are also to be grown in place. Samples of his brain and nerve tissue are extracted, sent to a clear sphere and grey-like matter is entered. After several minutes, they are returned. The cells patch into the existing brain and nerve endings. Minor electrical shocks are sent, and the signal patterns of the brain are shown on the screen.

A new eye emerges from a white cube and floats in an egg-shaped container. The egg is the shape of Wulin’s eye socket and merges into it. The skin melts and forms eye fluid. Nerve endings find each other and wrap, then melt into one.

Wulin speaks clearly now for the first time since losing his eye. "Dawn, I am feeling happy again. Thought I would never feel happy again, but for some reason, I feel very good."

Dawn says, "Wait, and soon you will be able to see with your new eye."

The computer surgery system now purges his blood of the damaged tissue. Electrical tests are conducted on his optical nerves and brain. The signal's pathways are shown to be in line with normal brain function. The eyelid is repaired. Nerve signals open the eyelid to reveal his new eye. Brown like his original eye, but shiny and clear of any discoloration.

His clothes materialize and are put on for him. Wulin is lifted to his feet.

Wulin stands and his arms are slowly released to his side. He looks around peacefully but does not know what happened or where he is.

Wulin speaks, "Excuse me, am I dreaming?

Dawn replies, "Your eye and brain damage caused by the operation to fit H33 with his rear-view sight have been corrected. How do you feel? Can you see well?"

Wulin says, "I feel very good and see extremely well. Am I drugged?"

"No and . . .Don't do drugs!" Dawn says, having copied a voice from the internet and laughing. "I also feel a lot better. Go home, Wulin and don't offer strangers any more organs!"

Wulin says, "I don't know the way home."

Dawn says, "Silly boy, I will fly you there."

They are in the space shuttle and flying over the mountains of deep China as farmers look up at the sky. They circle over his village, and people follow the ship to the back of Wulin's house, where his drones still lie partially assembled. Dawn looks over the circuits, analyzes them and sends electricity through them. She sees the problems and, instead of fixing them, sends Wulin the information directly to his brain.

Wulin says, "So that's the problem," he says, now realizing the solution.

Dawn says, "Have a happy life, kid."

She flies off, and Wulin waves and says, "I forgot to tell you to thank you and I love you for all you have done to give me my life back."

Dawn replies, "No worries. I also feel a lot better!"

H33 Prepares for His First Battle

H33 has been training hard with his full armament implanted and tested in simulated battles and against others like himself. His nervous system is fine tuned to exceed the response rate of any creature on Earth. His mind is sharp. Elizabeth has been working on his mental conditioning. Now it's time for his first real battle.

Huston speaks to H33, "You look impressive. Many improvements over H11 and H22. Is that a new eye?" as he jumps over H33, then flaps his wings to separate the hair to fully see the eye. The eye blinks from the wind of his wings. "Very fashionable. Does it provide the same visibility as your other eyes?"

H33 says, in his growling voice, "Yes, I think it looks amazing and don't you think it suits me? Visibility, well, that is military recognizance and top secret!"

Huston says, "The sense of humor on this planet is well developed. I think we should preserve it. Okay the fun is over, the fight is about to begin. The thought process in this next battle is key. Hope you have learned much from the previous encounters."

H33 roars like a lion, "YES."

Huston says, “Okay, then good luck. I see you are ready to go.” He shouts, imitating boxing announcers, “NOW ITTT’SSSS TIME!”

H33-1 BATTLE: Fog & Rock

H33 is in on a foggy planet and his visibility is low. He tries to use his bat-implanted radar, but it only shows a hard layer of uneven land ahead of him. He tries to see his hand in front of him, at first, nothing. His eyes try to adjust. He puts his hand inches away from his face. He can begin to see a blurred hand, but at full stretch, it disappears. He wonders around the uneven ground and hears nothing but his own footsteps that make a whooshing sound. He tries to keep silent. He decides to stop and listen. Hearing picks up the sound of a fast-moving object. It must be airborne.

Then he hears it coming, too late, it's too fast and slices across his arm and chest, leaving a large gash. Only his heavily armored body saves him. He hears the sound again, now jumps quickly aside and it just misses him. The speed is incredible. What strategy can he use? He must be able to catch and stop this creature so he can grab it. Otherwise, it will tear him apart. He moves quickly to a pile of rocks and stands beside it, making a concave shell. At that speed, it will not be able to hit him and avoid the surrounding rocks. He waits. His bleeding is slowing thanks to his genetic modifications. It comes in again just as fast; he moves just a few feet. It slashes off his arm and along with it, his shoulder, but then it crashes into the rocks. He grabs it by the neck with his other arm, it tries to fly away, but he directs it onto the rock and then pummels it with his knees, rocks behind the fly and he continues to pound it, getting on top and rolling it into the rocks. His sharp nails dig into its neck. It shrieks, a high-pitched scream damaging his hearing. He can no longer stand and rolls aside, holding the creature in his hand, bleeding badly but puts a knee into it. Then he pounds it with his other sharply pointed knee. He is bleeding badly and tries to stay conscious, but after a few hits passes out.

His body disappears as he is returned home. Back on Earth, people silently applaud his efforts as he had won. His body is moved into the operating room, where major surgery is underway.

Earth has its first win; people cheer worldwide. H33 is now everyone's hero. Cheering, is a thing of the past. Considered corny and in poor taste as it put down the other contestant. Now they don't care and embrace it, singing, "33, 33, 33, 3, 3. 33. 33 save me. 33 save me."

Just one week after his win, H33 is back in full form, working out in the Combatant gym. His strength and agility have returned. With his mental strength proven, he has added confidence. Confidence and intelligence are his key weapons allowing him to adapt quickly to the alien planets. Videos of his training sessions are shown around the world as the number one viewing program.

He is interviewed. “H33, how is your recovery and are you ready for your next battle?” from a middle-aged reporter with grey hair.

H33 speaks, “Well, I only had a scratch from the previous battle, so it hardly slowed me down. Stitched me up and I was ready to go. Battle-tested, I am all the more ready to go. Bring them on, one after the other. They are going down!”

H33-2 Battle Between the Twin Planets

H33 arrives on a planet like Earth but it is much smaller. The atmosphere is very thin and windy, swirling upward and downward as much as sideways. He finds himself very light on his feet. The ground is stable but not very firm. The sky color swirls between light brown and ash with green streaks. Hard to focus. Plants live like tumbleweeds. They are lush vines with ball-like leaves on a round core and many bent branches. Then he sees a large mass appearing off the horizon. Is it a moon, sun, or planet? It is very large, the same size as the planet he is on. But no real heat. It is a large moon, no – it is a twin planet. The sky seems to engulf it.

The wind picks up, and lots of plants are swirling around. The wind knocks him to the ground. He springs back up, inadvertently jumping very high. The gravity has been substantially affected by the approach of this near planet/moon. He runs away from it, but it catches up too fast. He crouches down in a defense position looking for his combatant. Can it be one of these plant creatures? No, there are too many, but he had been told that they could be plant-like. The twin planet passes over him. The sky is filled with plants that come from the twin planet and merge with those from the original one he stands on. Some plants brush against him; he protects himself with his huge arms. Checks for any damage. His skin hair raises in protection, many hairs are scraped off, but his skin is only slightly red. As the other planet passes over, objects start to fly at him at higher speed, making it dangerous to stay. He runs with the wind, picking up more and more speed. He jumps and travels high and far under the strong moon-like gravity from the other planet. He passes over a mound, jumps and gets very high. He sees other objects above him with higher speed go up and up towards the other planet. Maybe the wind and the gravity of the second planet pick them up. He lands. If he can master jumps around this planet and back, he may have a great advantage. He runs full speed now to match that of the wind and sees a large hill ahead. Other objects are being sent airborne. He jumps hard and up. He flies high, higher, air thinning, he starts to slow down, oh no, maybe he won't make it and fall hard, but then as he approaches zero vertical speed, he starts to accelerate towards the twin planet.

He fights to change his orientation towards the ground on the other planet. His eyes adjust, he uses his radar vision, he sees a creature, large flat like body in a 4-point stance, flat top, very strong and powerful looking, 4 arms and 4 eyes looking up and sideways. H33 grasps a flying plant. Then another, now he is camouflaged. He uses the plants and his body to sail towards the creature. The creature tries to stay on the ground, but the low gravity and high winds prevail and start to move it around uncomfortably. C3 is able to fly towards it and arranges himself to go in feet first. He lets go of the plant at the last possible moment. The creature sees him but too late. His sharp feet land before the center of its round back/head. They dig in slightly against the very tough skin. Then he uses his knees and elbow and finally drives in with his diamond fists, making a long hard hit on the creature. He ends up bouncing off, doing summersaults in the air and lands on the ground in a dive roll. The creature must be injured, but it is after him with rage and a low thundering roar. He begins to run away with the wind. As the other planet is moving away again, he jumps high to return. The creature tries to follow but is too big and slow, and with its large surface area, it is blown away back. H33 makes it back to the first planet.

He stops on land to think. Analyzes his view of the creature, round four legs and arms, like a trampoline but thick like a rhino. The feeling at contact was like Kevlar with heavy cartilage underneath. Vital organs must be protected underneath. His impact would have caused the equivalent of broken ribs and some internal bleeding, its weakened structure should result in slower movement. This is why its chase was slow and unorthodox. Trying to get underneath it would be very hazardous as it would put me within reach of its four arms and four legs. Another attack like the first would be expected and prepared for by the creature. What if he fakes an attack and then throws objects? If he comes in too low, it could jump to reach him. This would expose its underside to attack but also expose him to being captured by its immense strength. The safest way would be to throw projectiles; penetrating spears would be the best. The flying plants might make good spears. High-velocity rocks could also be used to flip it over and then the spears could penetrate its weaker underside.

Sounds like a good plan. He grabs several plants and opens up the inside of a large one to make a basket. He collects several large rocks. Making three spears from the branches, he then sharpens them with rocks. Primitive but safer than getting into its grasp. Then he adds camouflage to make it look like his first attack.

The planets align and he runs and jumps. He is making it over to the other planet but cannot find the creature. Maybe it dug a hole to hide and heal. Maybe it has its own new strategy – it must be very intelligent. He uses his radar vision and sees four evenly spaced plants not moving. It has turned over to hide and uses the plant to cover its attack. But with what attack mechanism? Does he assess how close he should get before throwing – rocks? Or spear? The creature moves to suck in its stomach. He throws his first heavy rock, and before it strikes, the creature spits something at him. It's a web entangling him while his heavy rock strikes one of his legs. He blocks the web with his basket, but it is acid and burns up the basket. He keeps one spear to try and ward off the web. He is half out, but it wraps up his legs and burns.

He cuts at it with his spear as he hits the ground. He tells himself to roll, roll, and the acid rubs off on the ground, minimizing the damage to his legs. He uses his spear to pull the rest of the web off his legs as his hands burn. He kneels down and rubs his hands on the ground. The creature moves towards him. His first spear is ruined, so he runs to find his other spear that landed fifty meters away. He dives to grab it and then stands and fires it at the creature. The spear gets stuck in one of its legs and renders it all but useless. They both stop and stare at each other. He grabs rocks and throws them at the injured leg. It turns to place the injured leg behind it. It has eyes on each of its four equal sides. It is ready for limb-to-limb combat. So is he. If he jumps high, it will turn over and shoot its acid web. On the ground, if it flips over, he knows what is coming and can quickly avoid it. He checks the damaged skin on his legs and hand but concludes it will not impede his movement. He has a mobility advantage over the large muscular foe with one damaged leg.

Speed kills. He is confident he can win this hand-to-hand even though his opponent is much larger and stronger. He will conceal his quickness until close by. He walks in slow, showing his strong muscles and toughness to let it think he will do battle based on strength. It moves in directly, also digging into the ground for force, leaving deep trenches with an alien grinding sound that starts like a rumble and ends high-pitched.

Now within 10 meters, its limbs are poise for an attack. He darts quickly to the right. It turns slightly, then he moves back to the left as it tries to turn back, digging in, then he jumps on top. It tries to flip on its back to fire a web, but he lands on its back. Then he digs in under its skin with his sharp titanium-tipped nails of his left hand and beats it with his diamond knuckles of his right hand. It flips on its back, burying him underneath. But the weak gravity is on his side and he is not crushed. He is able to push it off enough to start pummeling it again, breaking its cartilage. He digs in deeper with his left hand exposing its internals. The blood is acidic and burning, but his will is strong and this battle will be long over before the acid kills him.

The creature tries to rub him off like a bug on its back, but he had broken through its exterior. It spits out a web and tries to roll him onto it. It is successful and again, he is burning and entangled but keeps himself tight against its skin to minimize the damage to one side. This is a good trade-off of his superficial damage for its internal damage. He slices further in and starts to feel vital organs, cuts through one, then another, it roars, and then he feels something moving in a circular fashion - must be a rotary heart. He cuts it and squeezes it with his fingers. It stops moving. The moaning stops, but he does not assume it is dead. He continues to cut for more organs, then the creature makes a sudden jump up to land and squashes him. The force knocks the air out of his lungs, he tries to breathe, but it has dumped acid on him. Must hold my breath as this could kill me through my lungs. Now he puts both hands in to search for organs. He finds an egg-like shell, maybe the brain inside. Smashes at it and hears a crack, then he pierces inside and makes one final slice. The creature relaxes all its muscles. Then he pushes it off him, slices through the web, rolls away and keeps rolling. Smoke is coming off his skin, forming a putrid cloud of lime green gas. Now finally, he takes a deep breath, his lungs burn, but at least he can get some oxygen. He knees up in a defensive position to view the creature. It has died. He surveys his damage. His shark-like skin is smoldering but still has some thickness left. "Thank God for sharks," he says. Then he stands up tall and tilts his head towards the sky and sees the second planet moving away and the enormous and powerful foe on its back defeated and disappearing back to its planet, leaving him alone looking at a violent scene now transformed into one calm and beauty. This is a good trophy memory. And then he is whisked away back to Earth sooner than he would have liked.

Earth wins and people cheer worldwide. H33 is now everyone's hero and he stands upon a new winner's platform at the island where humans first met the 1000 species.

H33 Returns To the lab

The 1000 species return H33 to the operating room, where his skin is steaming from the acid. He is immediately placed in a milk-like bath to neutralize the acid. The composition of the acid is analyzed, and the molecular structure is not from Earth, so chemists analyze it to determine why it is so caustic. The bath is drained and fresh water with varying neutralizing agents is added to maximize the PH neutralization. H33's skin deterioration is monitored, and the scientists finally start to see neutralization of the acid. High-speed flow is used to cleanse his deep wounds. Then he is placed in a healing bath to replenish his skin. His lung tissue is evaluated microscopically, and the damaged sections removed by micro robots and embryonic cells are added to grow new tissue. After a few weeks, he is out walking and retraining lightly.

Then he meets with Elizabeth to review his mental strength.

Post Event Analysis With Elizabeth

What do you think about when not in battle? She asks.

H33 says, "You mean like right now? I can't stop thinking about how to kill something."

Elizabeth replies, "You mean even people?

H33 says, "Yes and how to kill as quickly as possible. Even you initially, but that is old now. Not with anger but just analytically. Even ants, but imagine them much bigger than me and many of them working jointly. Same for very large insects. When I pass a dog, I look at how it is growling at me, how it would attack, and how I would counterattack or attack first. Hard for me to think about mundane things versus life and death battles."

Elizabeth asks, "Is there anything that gives you pleasure."

H33 starts off slow, and his power of speech increases as he says, "The massage and added nutrients, but eating is of little pleasure via tubes and intravenous injections. An operation with new weapons or defense is very satisfying, like being a fighter jet with a new weapons bay. In the gym, the power, speed, analysis, feedback, backup systems and biology are involved. All that science and POWER is very satisfying."

Elizabeth asks, "What about Serenity?"

H33 replies, "She is great. She helps me relax and asks nothing of me. Just serves me what I need."

Elizabeth shows a slight sign of jealousy but subdues it quickly. "She provides you with the physical support?"

H33 replies, "Yes, mental too. Not in-depth like you, but helps me turn off. Just watching her work is a pleasure."

Elizabeth asks, "Do you find her beautiful?"

H33 replies, "Yes, but the doctors turned off my sexual drive. Just as well, it would probably kill her or anyone else."

Elizabeth asks, "What about your other drive?"

H33 replies, "Oh, I have lots of drive in another direction."

Elizabeth says, "Describe it to me."

H33 replies, "Do I have to?"

Elizabeth says, "I think it would help me help you and help yourself."

H33 says, "Well, I am a killer."

Elizabeth replies, "Yes, we know."

H33 speaks, "Well, actually, you don't. I have this power, and I want to use it to kill all the time, everything and everyone."

She is a bit scared but trying not to show it. "Deep down, I know you to be a good person, sacrificing your life to save us all."

H33 replies, “Yes, I feel good, wish to save our race, but also have this need to kill. It must be the conditioning and the implants from killer species. A thirst for blood and to even eat my kill, but this also grosses me out, so I will not. The scientists have done a lot for me. I hardly remember what I was like before, not that this is important. If I don’t keep winning, it is all for not. Don’t expect my life to be long. But much better than being on the sidelines and watching our fate unfold, powerless, doing nothing. How do these people cope with just being on the sidelines, watching and waiting for the end?”

Elizabeth speaks, “They deal with lots of despair, use family, friends, and we all try to stay optimistic that our scientists and intellect and ah, leadership, will turn the corner and convince the 1000 species that we deserve the planet. But back to you. You have been in a battle. What was that like?”

H33 says, “I hardly remember, my mind was so focused, in the zone, primitive and calculating all the options for attack, defense, analyzing the opponent, the planet. So much mental work is going on at the limit of my brain capacity. And then I felt I was dying but still fighting and thinking about how to win. Afterward, more mentally exhausted than physically. I rejuvenate quickly after the operations.”

Elizabeth says, “Okay, let me take you through the mental rejuvenation techniques I have devised for you. Put on this headset, and you will have sights, sounds, smells and a massage to put your mind in a state of meditation that will relax all synapses. Focus on your achievements as a whole. Not just the win but all that you have accomplished in your training. The operations are also an achievement. Relax into a meditation of the feeling of accomplishing a great task.”

He puts them on and sees a range of pastel colors fading to light green, soft smells of essential oils, a warm massage of his neck and skull, and a comforting speech stating that all his training and dedication have paid off with the biggest win of Earth’s history and he is responsible for this great win and can now rest and heal from the battle in a deep sleep, satisfied that he has more than fulfilled his task. He brings back the vision of the dual planets and the calm wind as he stands tall, and the lime green gas fades into a pale blue cloud.

Sam's Insights

Sam provides a short history of his species 1000 to a group of intellectual scientists, philosophers, a few political leaders, and Lucille, the agent for change.

Sam says, "Our species, like many others, had to fight for planet dominance, unlike yours where you were clearly the dominant and most intelligent. Instead, you fought within your own species. This distinction over other Earth-born species is possibly alien or a genetic mutation; given that humans are not happy with native Earth and reform it. A lack of harmony is prevalent. You cannot say that humans are home building while preserving nature. In our species 1000 history, an advanced race visited our planet and gave us some advice and technology. They then disappeared from our known universe. Extrapolation of their direction and philosophy suggests they propelled themselves to the frontiers of universe expansion, where they became the children of the new. Always in a state of wonder, one with the birth of the universe, like a child constantly excited about universe creations and learning at a rapid pace. No responsibilities or burdens. Just watching the universe unfold, enjoying firsts every moment. Perspective. Try to expand beyond the short term and find your own view of the future."

H33-3: High Gravity

H33 awakes pinned to the ground. Breathing is very difficult, slow and forced. Is his breathing apparatus faulty? Did the Aliens screw up?

Huston speaks directly to his mind, “Of course not. You have plenty of O2. Think again.”

So, he does. Tries to move his hands, which is very difficult. He can’t lift them legs also. Oh, gravity must be very strong here. He rolls his head to the side; this he can do. Everything is very flat on this planet, smooth like a billiard ball. The planet is very large, judging by the very flat horizon. The sky is clear with no wind. No hills, no rocks. Polished by the extreme gravity. He continues to force his breathing. His eyesight is adjusting. Wait, he sees something moving from the eye in the back of his head. It looks like a pool of liquid. Oh crap, it is moving towards him, and he cannot move.

This must be the competition. He sees the pool of liquid has an eye. If it rolls on him, it will squash him and suffocate him. He thinks: What options do I have? I can roll my head. Now let me see, yes, I can roll my hand now, max effort and I can now roll my arm but barely lift it. Even rolling my feet to the side is possible. But I cannot sit up.

The pool creature is inching towards him. His heart rate has elevated to the max, but he cannot breathe any faster, or he will be exhausted from the immense gravity. Must relax to keep my body in check. The pool creature is now next to him. It's hot, now moving over his leg, crushing it with agony; he wiggles his foot and the jagged toenails cut into the creature and it moves off his foot. Now it is on his right arm and crushing it. He rotates his hand up, cutting with his nails and slicing back and forth. The creature's eye is now close to his head; he can look into it and see cells of golden mud with several dots. If he can just roll over onto it. His right side is pinned and getting crushed. This allows him to roll his left arm over himself. He breathes into its eye. It closes, then he rolls his head over and bites the eye. It burns his mouth and he spits it out the half-chewed eye. It goes back into its pool. He has his left arm over it and rolls his fingers to dig in. Moving his fingers, he cuts sideways into it. With his body half crushed, he pushes the ground with his left hand to roll over onto it. He is now on his side, half over it, but his rib cage cannot take the gravity on its side and is getting crushed. His heart is failing along with the backup. There is the other eye and a series of veins to what might be organs. He opens his burning mouth and bites into it as he passes out in one last attempt.

Earthlings watch the scene viewing a messy mix of body and mud cells oozing away. The eye is crushed on the creature and one last breath of our hero comes out as a fine mist.

H33 awakens on an operating room table, alive. He had won by putting his mass on top, but barely.

After a week of operations and a drug-induced coma, the surgeons arrive and reverse the coma. They have replaced the crushed side of his body and it shines with new, improved skin. A doctor in the background watching vital signs announces, “He is awake!”

H33’s eyes move quickly from side to side and his mouth opens to suck in more air from the breathing apparatus.

The Head surgeon says, “You won, you can relax. We have patched you up and made some improvements. Your bones now have added strength and improved ductility so they will flex without being crushed so easily.”

H33 speaks, “I won? Didn’t think so. I don’t recall jumping for joy, fist-pumping, or making a signature move.”

Head surgeon with a sense of humor, “Only two of the three judges gave you the split decision. If you keep getting better, maybe your next battle will be a KO.”

H33 gets up slowly from the table and looks at the surgeons and the apparatus. Then he looks at his own body, “So this is new, and this is new too. Ok”. He moves his new arm, and it moves quicker than expected. “Twitchy, hmm, I like it. I will need to get accustomed to my new digs.”

He stands up, checks his balance, then sees a rack of clothes near the exit. “Not much selection in this store, but at least they have my size. He steps into the shoes that open as his foot approaches and then close snuggly. The pants are open at the back; he slaps them on his legs and they close up along the back. Tight fit but very stretchy. The hoody is old school, so he pulls it over his head. Then he tells the surgeons, “I am released!” and walks out.

Serenity is there to meet him outside and walks beside him without saying a word. The corridor is cleared via red light warnings ahead of them but turns off as they approach.

Just before they walk outside, Serenity tries to jump up and pull his hoody over his head. After the second attempt, H33 stops and says, “Do I look that bad?” and smiles. “You could have just asked.” Then he flips his head forward and the hood goes over his head.

Serenity speaks, “You are very famous, you know. People will stare.”

H33 says, “I will stare back at the first one, then it will stop.”

As they walk outside, they look up at the sky billboard projections created by lasers on water vapor and dust particles. H33 images in battle are shown pointing out the skill, biology, and capabilities that helped him win. Doctors in lab coats discuss the requirements to improve his weakness. A young man walks by and looks at his face. He is shocked to see who he is and gasps. Before H33 can stare at him, he bows his head and walks away discretely.

One month later, he is back in top form, working out in the enhanced gym with varying gravity levels and atmosphere densities.

The head coach approaches him, “H33, your next challenge is coming!”

“Great, the training is starting to get old,” H33 replies.

Trainers and medical staff nearby are astounded that he is still excited to do battle after his near-death experiences. H33 sees their expressions and roars out like a lion, “Not human in this regard. My predatory instincts overwhelm any desire to sit idle. Fighting to the death is WHAT I LIVE FOR!”

H33-4 Gas Planet Conflict

H33 arrives on the planet and floats on dense gas that somehow holds his weight.

Huston appears, "As you can see, dense gas can behave like a solid as long as it is significantly denser than you. 61% of planets are gas planets and many have life forms. You will now experience one. Semi-solid versus dense gas. Good luck –I don't know why Humans say good luck, but it provides a nice closure to the conversation."

H33 watches his hands disappear in a dense cloud. He feels the friction of the gas against his skin. He is accelerating deeper into the gas planet. The friction on his skin starts decreasing until he is moving at the same speed as the gas. His eyes adjust to the gas and now he sees layers of different gas colors above and below him. The gases move at slightly different speeds. Above him, the gases become violet, then pink and finally white. Below him, the violet turns to blues, then fades to black. He experiments by moving his hand upward into the faster moving gas above him. This begins to turn him, so he puts his hand down and places it below him. His rotation is reversed. Now he swims himself upward, but when he stops swimming, he falls back to his original level. This must mean that the gas density at this level is equal to his density.

He takes a deep breath and realizes that he has some kind of invisible breathing apparatus making the cloud feel like air back home. Then he notices that breathing requires more effort due to the higher gas density, but the oxygen intake is the same. Wait, he tells himself, I have two lungs and can breathe from one at a time. Should have tested the air on one side first, but I trust Huston not to suffocate me. H33 remembers his training and how his intake manifolds had restricting his breathing. The scientists gave him a double barrel intake using embryo technology to make him a second windpipe.

The mind must focus on my prey, he thinks. He scans the cloud vapors for signs of life. None. Any signs of gas discontinuity? Colors vary with altitude but radially… then he is hit by a wave of gas that surprises him. He takes a defensive position with his arms and legs bent in front of him. He felt a definite pressure pulse but is that atmospheric or life? It didn't hurt, suggesting atmospheric. He focuses in the circumferential direction and uses his back eye as well. Now he sees a jellyfish in the shape of a circular ameba with hair-like tentacles. Actually, more like a ghost, but making analogies is fruitless, he thinks. It throws all of its tentacle hairs backward and it propels itself at him. He tries to move out of the way but can only turn. It strikes him but goes through and around him. Again, no damage that he can detect, just a wave of warm gas. It turns and attacks again.

This time, he swings at it with both arms and legs. No effect. Then he swims at it and tries to grab hold of it, only to have it flow through his hands.

This can go on and on, H33 thinks. Then it attacks his nose, trying to get inside him. His breathing is blocked, so he exhales sharply and waves it off with his hands, then blocks his nose. But it tries to enter his mouth and ears and even his eyes, so he closes his eyes and wraps his hands around his ears but cannot block all passages. His mind races at full speed, trying to come up with options to defeat it. He kicks his feet to move it away, and it has some effect, but the creature can move more effectively and moves back around it and attacks his breathing passages and ear holes.

Think fast!

Only one option can he devise. He has two lungs and can block off the entrance to either one with his tongue. Maybe he can suck part of the creature into one of his lungs and then trap it while breathing through the other lung. It attacks his face once more, and then he takes a deep breath into his right lung, and when it is full, he blocks the entrance with his tongue and mouth, cutting it with his teeth. The creature is hurt and squirms with the part in his lungs trying to fight its way out. It wraps itself around him, trying to reunite the two parts. H33 waves it off with his feet and one hand. It tries to enter his mouth, but he holds tight with one hand over his nose. It tries to enter his ears and creates sharp pain in his ear drums. He hears a loud gas rushing sound. He has been holding his breath but now breathes slowly into his other lung to keep himself from passing out. He can feel the creature in his lung pulsing like it is breathing or beating. He decides to try and crush it and uses his core strength to press his lung closed and sucks the right side of his stomach into his chest. He does this and starts to fall to a lower level in the atmosphere. The remainder of the creature tries to follow him but must work hard to lower itself into the increased density. Injured, it starts to head back upward. H33 swims hard downward. He continues to collapse his one lung with the alien inside while breathing through the other lung.

It is getting darker at the lower levels. The creature portion in his lung is causing him great discomfort – why? His lung starts to convulse. Can't hold it in any longer and it spits out the creature along with blood from his lung. The blood and the high density make the remains of the half creature dissipate into globules mixed with his blood. Expanding his lungs, H33 floats back up. He sees the remainder of the creature. Is it still alive? Can it function without 40% of its mass? As H33 moves in for the kill, it moves slowly away. He takes a deep breath to threaten it and the creature begins to expand. He moves his hands to spread the remains of the gas alien and it dissipates.

"I call that a KO!" shouts H33.

Huston appears in the gas, “Smart move, sacrificing one lung.”

H33 says, “Yeah, that is what I did.” and thinks to himself, not on purpose, though.

Houston says, “I heard that, you know. More importantly, that is four. Count them, four wins in a row. You are highly adaptive to your new planetary surroundings and quickly analytical. Humans have done well to embrace Earth’s rich biological resources. Time to take over a continent on another planet. Would you like to see the menu?”

H33 says, “Is Hawaii or Australia on the menu?”

Houston says, “Sorry, H33, those seats have been taken. You don’t want to go back to your old ways, do you?”

Houston speaks, “May I suggest from the menu? Q*(19763) with 27% H2O surface, it is the next highest in the galaxy. Located, well, very far away. Not a weekend stop. Current habitats are somewhat humanoid. They are also not great at self-management.”

H33 says, “Second choice?”

Houston replies, “10% surface H20 mix with sulfuric acid. Lakes, you would not want to put your toe in it.”

H33 says, “Tell the restaurant owner he needs to work on the menu. I prefer the home-cooked option.”

Houston says, “Cooking at home; then you need to do the dishes! Not a popular activity on Earth.”

A year passes. H33 and the human race enjoy victory and Australia and Hawaii are returned to humans. Learning from the alien forms, they keep much of their improvements but return the vegetation to earth’s original species. History of vegetation and native species are now taught in primary school. H33 is tired of being a celebrity, hates it and the need to fight is running in his veins. Asks for more battles, then begs for more.

Another battle is looming. The chief trainer has many new younger, stronger contestants. H33 has the most experience but is his age and his many injuries a handicap or an advantage?

They ask H33.

H33 looks left, right and then right at them. “You dare to ask this stupid question? Have you been paying attention? Have you lost it? Are your noses in your lab coats and formulas? Surely you get it by now. It's not strength and speed. It’s the mind that wins. Which of these men can you guarantee will stay sharp and analytically calm to search for a win when they have a dagger in their heart? When they have lost their legs, bleeding from many sites, heart racing to stay alive, adrenalin spikes to flight or fight, instead of quick analytical thinking of scenarios to win. This can’t be taught. There can be no fear of death, or shame of loss, or worries about the impact to Earth. The only question that arises in me? How can I beat this alien at this instant?"

The chief trainer takes a deep breath and steps back in his defense. "Just what we needed to hear. Still hungry to step into the battle zone. And you don't want to relinquish the title."

H33 says, "Please give the title to one of them to prance around the globe. Appearances and speeches are not for me. What happens when you put a line in a cage in front of an audience? Does it want to poise, make a roar? No, it wants to eat everyone. You put that animal instinct in me. So far, I have fought off the urge. Now, I am at my limit."

The Chief trainer says, "You, back to the gym, no more talk. You are on deck for the next battle!"

H33 says, "Now that's what I want to hear. Dam excellent news. On my way, make it ready."

H33-5 Battle is a Puzzle

Houston says, “Hey, it’s you again. H33, I thought you retired? (that should stimulate a response from my studies of humanity)”

H33 asks, “Do you know the phrase, ‘piss off’?”

Houston replies, “Yes, it worked. Humans are predictable. Okay, my new friend, we have an interesting challenge for you. This next life form is more developed than the others. A whole new challenge. Good luck.”

H33 flexes his muscles, and fades away, then appears in a new colorless world.

H33 thinks, *on solid ground, bounce, light gravity 0.6Gs, bounce some more, light flex in surface, stuff on the ground, some growing off it, some floating above it, a breeze of gas with light objects floating by. The eyes cannot focus as everything has either no color or a mix of changing unstable colors. Can see objects, okay. Let me touch some floating objects. They deflect off my fingers. No effect on my skin. Touch the ground. It stops my hand, I can press on it, but no feeling of any kind just stops me. How can that be? Is this a computer simulation? The objects coming from the ground are like flat blades of grass with pouches that catch the floating objects, feeding off them, I guess. Let’s hit one. Sound wave pressure on my ears but without tone. Well, I am not calibrated for this planet. Is it round and large?*

Horizon? No horizon? Let's walk in one direction, Nothing, running, nothing. The sky and ground just seem to merge into one with no horizon line. I guess the planet's atmosphere is too thick. Where does the light come from? Seems to come from everywhere and nowhere. Presume that the atmosphere is thick and diffuses the light.

H33 continues thinking, *any signs of my opponent? Visibility is one kilometer. Nothing. No danger. Will just wait and adjust to this. Look around, turn 180 degrees, then steps of 90 degrees. I will start hiking in the direction of a brighter side of this planet. Hills become steeper, vegetation changes, now some kind of fruit trees, something growing from the ground, some fluid running down hills. Some pale colors appear.*

Days go by with the light changing to darkness. Each night is getting progressively darker. H33 starts to suffer from fatigue from lack of water or food.

Then he sees it, footsteps or dragged steps. Three drag lines with alternating gaps. He follows them. Then starts to run. The lines get further apart. The creature must now be running. He runs faster, lines get further apart. After several hours he slows down. Needs to find rest and shelter. Test the ground, it is safe and flat. He decides to sleep between two tree-like blades. It should be free of falling leaves here and still provide some protection.

He falls asleep. After a few hours, he senses something, jumps up alert looks around. Something moves quickly away. There is a pool of liquid to his right on the ground. He runs to see the object but cannot find a trail. Returns back to look at the liquid. Clear substance, water-like but thick and viscous. Could it be poison? He tries to smell it. Nothing. Touches it with his left 5th finger. Nothing. It was not there when he went to sleep. Did it rain or perspire from the tree grass? Checks the tree grass, it's dry. So he squeezes it and fluid drops from it. It's the same fluid. Should I dare taste it? Very thirsty. Will try a small drop. Puts his finger in it, then puts it in his mouth. No taste but refreshing. Waits for his body to react. It likes it. Takes a sip. Refreshing. Waits, nothing but refreshing. Takes a good slip. Not bad.

H33 starts hiking uphill. He is looking for higher ground for a view to see if he can find his enemy. He sees the three drag trails crossing in front of him. He takes a line to cut it off and runs at full speed, dodging between the grass trees. He sees a creature, long and thin, with three legs that bend continuously like blades of grass that spring it forward very fast. It doesn't seem him coming. He can cut it off. Getting close, I can jump it. He springs up and at it, but it carefully turns away and he misses. It must have seen him coming and quickly escapes.

Thirsty, he grabs some of the grass trees and squeezes to extract the fluid. Now he gets his full. Nourishing and thirst quenching.

Getting dark, he finds a place against a rock-like hill. He sits up against the wall for defense. It becomes very dark and he falls asleep.

"What's that? There it is again." He jumps up, see something move and throws his rock-like objects. Runs out to see. Nothing, same three drag lines on the ground. Follows them, but then they disappear. He goes back to where he was sleeping. His remaining rock-like objects are gone. Instead, there is something on the ground. It's a net from a plant that collects airborne objects. Inside a flower-like ball that has been broken in a tri hub fracture. Inside a purple-like granular substance.

"Now I know the creature left the water-like fluid for me, took my weapons and left me this substance. It must be a trap to get my confidence to eat this poison and kill me. This is a puzzle. Do I simply walk away, learn nothing, or take a risk to analyze it? The creature could have attacked me or put the poison on me or close to me. It also has not attacked me.

I DON'T GET IT! Think, what the hell is happening here! I am going to test this substance safely. Get a long blade from the tree and stick it into the purple stuff. He does it. Nothing, wait, the blade is turning lighter and starting to grow ever so slightly. Okay, let me smell it from a distance.

Wave my hand towards my nose and feel some light pressure, but nothing.

Crap! Now I have to taste it. Touch it first, nothing. Smell again. Pleasant. Minute on my finger, nothing. Okay, smallest of taste. Somewhat pleasant. Almost wish it was poison so I can make sense of this. Try a bit more. God, it feels good. Feeling instant energy. I really want to eat a lot. Okay, take some and wait. Feeling a lot better. It's like drug food. Damn good. Okay, now I am going to eat a lot. Wow, that is good and now some water from the tree grass. Energy level going back to 90%. Time to sit down and think. A creature teaches me about water and food and takes my weapons but does not attack. Is it my opponent or an innocent third party with a big heart? Houston said it was advanced. Is it playing mind games? I face no threats from an opponent or the environment. My sense to kill is inactive."

H33 stops and thinks in silence for one hour in meditation.

He remembers his history. What he was like before all the procedures. Then the aliens arrive first, threatening all humans. He is called to action in defense. He kills after being given the sense to fight for self-preservation and for food from his animal instincts. Now he faces a species trying to help him.

"Why fight, why kill? Who tells me to kill the innocent? Why do I listen? I don't have the right to kill this species if it is helping me. Damn me if I do. What are my options here? Puzzle, if we don't fight, there is no winner. It's a draw. I will make a big pool of water and some food. Make a big sign and leave it for the other guy. Sit back at a distance and watch."

He makes a nice setting, a pool of water like his first, food broken open like he found it but two of them. Then three big grass leaves in the shape of the trails he chased.

He sits back on a hill about 300 meters away but with his back protected. No weapons. Waits.

He sees the creature approach. Then it goes off to one side, then the other. Then it approaches his gifts. It looks at it, touches it, smells it, tastes it. Just like he did, obviously imitating H33.

Then it looks up at him. Walks halfway to him. Then bows down on two legs with his head down and waits.

H33 is now at his limit. This is going too well, too fast, too much of a departure from his battles to the death. But it feels really good.

"I will take the risk of going towards it, but just halfway."

He walks slowly toward it. It continues to bow down. Not looking at him. He is now 100 meters away and stops and takes a knee. He waits. It waits.

Then it slowly looks up at him. They look at each other. His heart races. It looks slightly alarming. Calming, he lowers his heart rate. It looks more relaxed now. It sits. He sits.

They wait, after several hours. It points to the food and bows to him. He points to it and bows to it. The creature slowly sides toward the food on the far side and waves him to come.

"Am I really going to eat dinner with this creature? Yes, I am," he smiles.

They sit next to each other in front of the food.

"I point to it to eat. It points to me to eat. Well, let's both eat at the same time," and they begin.

They finish the food and then look at each other.

The creature bows to him, and he bows back. Then he sees the creature start to disappear, and his hands and body also start to disappear.

Houston appears in front of him and he is back on earth on the beach where they first met the aliens 1000.

Houston says, "Amazing, I have just witnessed the next step of the evolution of humanity. Dude, what did you just do?"

H33 says, "No one tells H33 to kill for no reason. Not even a 1000 species kid. I make my own decisions and will not be a murderer anymore."

Houston asks, "How does it feel to evolve?"

H33 says, “Amazing feeling of freedom and self-purpose. Like no one can tell me what to do anymore.”

Houston says, “You really got it then. Amazing. All of Earth witnessed this evolution. There will be no more wars on this planet if this evolution grows in the mind of humanity.”

H33 replies, “I think I want to make appearances, maybe even a speech.”

Houston says, “Go for it. Great work out there. Did it hurt to evolve?”

H33 says, “Yes, never been so scared. Torn inside between fighting and… you know, I don’t even know what to call what I did.”

Houston says, “Plenty of time to name it. Just keep doing it and this place will be all right again.”

Final Comments

Sam to the world over every device.

"You are part of the universe, created by it. To have a glimpse of the universe, you can look within yourself. If you dream it, then the universe has already created it, within you and elsewhere. After all, it is infinite. If there is one Big Bang, as you call it, then there is an infinite number of Big Bangs. The infinity concept cannot be fully appreciated by a land-based two-dimensional species on a finite world with a finite life horizon. As a result, your culture is short-term focused. Once one embraces infinity and that you are children of the universe, then this realization will transfer your belief to a higher and more satisfying purpose. You are one with the universe, created by it, ruled by its forces. You also evolve and expand with it. Attempt to be a bigger part of it and find harmony with its direction, a direction that none of us can change. You need to have a higher level of purpose, to survive and grow as one race. Everyone should have a place and purpose for this common goal. Lack of this results in unfulfillment in life and stress without resolution. Today you only have a goal for more wealth, yet those who achieve it seem to be the least happy and die young. Still, most strive for this, knowing deep down that this is not happiness. H33 showed you that even fighters could not be told to kill. They can make their own decisions now. Good moral decisions. No one can tell them or bully them into doing immoral acts. All humans need to evolve to this level. We see promise and hope that the Human race can make the leap, but time is quickly running out."

Dawn, Huston and JD fly down next to Sam. They face the world. Then jump up instinctively at the same instant and fly back over one of the last remaining rain forests, skimming the trees, and then turn up sharply towards their spaceship and disappear.

THE END.

www.ingramcontent.com/pod-product-compliance
Lightning Source LLC
LaVergne TN
LVHW050551160826
845677LV00011B/2262

9798848166545